www.penguin.co.uk

By Michael McDowell

THE BLACKWATER SAGA
Blackwater I: The Flood
Blackwater II: The Levee
Blackwater III: The House
Blackwater IV: The War
Blackwater V: The Fortune
Blackwater VI: Rain

The Amulet
Cold Moon Over Babylon
Gilded Needles
The Elementals
Katie
Toplin
Wicked Stepmother (with Dennis Schuetz)
Blood Rubies (with Dennis Schuetz)

THE FORTUNE

BLACKWATER V

MICHAEL McDOWELL

PENGUIN BOOKS

TRANSWORLD PUBLISHERS
Penguin Random House, One Embassy Gardens,
8 Viaduct Gardens, London SW11 7BW
www.penguin.co.uk

Transworld is part of the Penguin Random House group of companies
whose addresses can be found at global.penguinrandomhouse.com

Originally published in six volumes by Avon Books 1983
Published in one volume by Valancourt Books 2017
Blackwater V: The Fortune first published in Great Britain
in 2024 by Penguin Books
an imprint of Transworld Publishers

Copyright © The Estate of Michael McDowell 1983
This edition is published in agreement with Valancourt Books, LLC
through Piergiorgio Nicolazzini Literary Agency (PNLA).

Michael McDowell has asserted his right under the Copyright,
Designs and Patents Act 1988 to be identified as the author of this work.

This book is a work of fiction and, except in the case of historical fact,
any resemblance to actual persons, living or dead, is purely coincidental.

Every effort has been made to obtain the necessary permissions with
reference to copyright material, both illustrative and quoted. We apologize
for any omissions in this respect and will be pleased to make the
appropriate acknowledgements in any future edition.

A CIP catalogue record for this book
is available from the British Library.

ISBN 9781804996416

Cover illustration: © Pedro Oyarbide & Monsieur Toussaint Louverture.
Typeset in 11.25/15.25 pt Sabon by Falcon Oast Graphic Art Ltd.
Printed and bound in Great Britain by Clays Ltd, Elcograf S.p.A.

The authorized representative in the EEA is Penguin Random House Ireland,
Morrison Chambers, 32 Nassau Street, Dublin D02 YH68.

No part of this book may be used or reproduced in any manner
for the purpose of training artificial intelligence technologies
or systems. In accordance with Article 4(3) of the DSM
Directive 2019/790, Penguin Random House expressly reserves
this work from the text and data mining exception.

Penguin Random House is committed to a sustainable
future for our business, our readers and our planet. This book
is made from Forest Stewardship Council® certified paper.

For Mama El

The maenad loves – and furiously defends herself against love's importunity. She loves – and kills. From the depths of sex, from the dark, primeval past of the battles of the sexes arise this splitting and bifurcating of the female soul, wherein woman first finds the wholeness and primal integrity of her feminine consciousness. So tragedy is born of the female essence's assertion of itself as a dyad.

Vyacheslav Ivanov,
'The Essence of Tragedy'
(tr. Laurence Senelick)

I will spunge out the sweetness of my heart,
And suck up horror; Love, woman's thoughts,
    I'll kill,
And leave their bodies rotting in my mind,
Hoping their worms will sting; not man outside,
Yet will I out of hate engender much:
I'll be the father of a world of ghosts
And get the grave with carcase.

Thomas Lovell Beddoes,
'Love's Arrow Poisoned'

AUTHOR'S NOTE

Perdido, Alabama, does indeed exist, and in the place I have put it. Yet it does not now, nor ever did possess the buildings, geography, or population I ascribe to it. The Perdido and Blackwater rivers, moreover, have no junction at all. Yet the landscapes and persons I describe, I venture to say, are not wholly imaginary.

Please be aware that this book was originally written in the 1980s to depict the American Deep South of the 1950s, and therefore contains language, themes or characterizations that are reflective of that time.

ASSESSMENT

All the Caskeys sincerely mourned the death of James Caskey. Though the man had been old and frail, no one had imagined that he would ever die. He had been the oldest of the clan, though never in any sense its leader. Perhaps if he had been in a more exalted position, everyone would have wondered, *Who'll take over when James is gone?* But in fact, with his death there was no reshuffling of state and station, only an acknowledgment of the emptiness he had left behind.

Queenie was the one who felt most alone, and everyone treated her as if she had been a widow rather than James's sister-in-law. Her son Danjo was now married, but stuck in Germany with his German wife, unable to return because of difficulties with immigration – or so he wrote to his mother. Queenie's daughter Lucille had turned into the perfect 'farm wife' and had no use for a life in town with her mother. Her elder boy Malcolm, whom she hadn't seen since he ran away in 1938, she presumed to be dead.

The often volatile Lucille, in a sympathetic frame of mind, said, 'Ma, come out to the Pond and live with Grace and Tommy Lee and me.' Queenie merely shook her head, and wiped away a tear.

Sister said, 'Queenie, come next door and put up in Mary-Love's old room. I need me some company with Miriam over at the mill all day.' Queenie silently declined.

Elinor said, 'You know you're welcome with us.'

Queenie turned down all offers, and at last ventured a diffident request: 'Would it be all right if I just stayed on here? And took care of all James's old stuff? He loved this house so much!'

After a minimum of discussion, the family decided that it was the perfect solution, and Queenie's old house a few blocks away, which for a couple of years had been vacant most of the time, was sold.

James's daughter Grace had assumed that her father would leave the whole of his fortune to her – that was the way of the Caskeys – and she had been trying to figure out how best to distribute portions of that wealth to those who had been dear to her father. She was relieved at the reading of the will to discover that this would not be necessary. Except for some small bequests to his cook Roxie and to the Methodist Church of Perdido, James's entire fortune was divided equally among Queenie, Danjo, and Grace.

The trouble was, no one knew the extent of James's fortune. Yet this lack of knowledge proved to be the solution to another Caskey problem. Ever since Billy Bronze and Frances Caskey had got married, Billy had had a great deal of time on his hands, particularly after he was released from the Air Corps. He volunteered his services to the local Veterans Administration office and four evenings a week taught radio and accounting to ex-servicemen who drifted back to Perdido. But most of the time Billy felt useless, left alone all day with the women while his father-in-law Oscar and his sister-in-law Miriam went off to the bustling mill. He had declined an offer to work at the mill because he knew nothing of the lumber business. He understood that Oscar had made the job proposal only out of charity. Miriam, speaking with greater candor, had said: 'We'll be glad to put you on the payroll as long as you promise not to go out and get in everybody's way.' Billy wanted not only to work, but to work at something useful.

Frances, however, liked having her husband at home all day. She enjoyed the fact that he could drive her to Pensacola for an afternoon movie or down to Mobile for some shopping. But she saw also that he was restless. One morning in the winter of 1946, as

Frances and Billy lay in bed together, Frances turned to her husband and said, 'Maybe Miriam could find you a place in the office at the mill. I know you don't know anything about trees, and you don't like working out-of-doors, but you're fine with a pencil and an adding machine.'

'No, no,' protested Billy, 'don't do that! Please don't say anything to Miriam!'

'Why not?' asked Frances, puzzled.

'Just think for a minute,' said Billy. 'Just think how hard Miriam works at that mill.'

'She runs it!' said Miriam's sister proudly.

'That's just it,' nodded Billy. 'Now what do you think would happen if I suddenly started to show up there every day?'

'You'd help her run it better.'

Billy shook his head. 'No, no. Don't forget that I'm a Caskey now. So if I went to work in that office, people would start coming to me because I'm older – and because I'm a man. Pretty soon I'd have more power than Miriam, not because I was any better than her at it, but just because I was a man. Miriam knows that, and she doesn't want me there. And I don't blame her for one minute.'

'You think that's what would happen?'

'I know it,' returned Billy definitely. 'I am *not* going to interfere with your sister. She has worked long and hard. *But*,' said Billy, taking Frances in his arms, and pressing her head against his bare chest, 'maybe what I could do . . .'

'What?'

'I could keep books. That's what I do best.'

'But you just said that you didn't want to interfere—'

'I'm not talking about the mill,' said Billy. 'I'm talking about keeping books for the family, being a kind of personal accountant for everybody.'

'You think you could do that? Daddy says that everything's so confused.'

'I could do it without giving it a second thought. I inherited that from my father. Keeping books is how he made all his money. He was so good at it. At night he'd go down to his office and look through the books for ten minutes. Next day he'd go out and make five thousand dollars. I never saw anything like it.'

Frances was so excited by the idea that she pulled her husband out of bed and hurried him down to the breakfast room. She then insisted that he explain his proposal to Elinor and Oscar.

'Let me look things over,' Billy said. 'We ought to be able to figure out just what everybody's got. It wouldn't be a bad thing to find out what kind of shape you're all in.'

'Not a bad idea,' said Oscar, 'but I don't know where to tell you to begin, everything's so mixed up. See, we did pretty badly in the first years of the Depression and pretty well during the war. Then everybody was dying for a while, and there were wills to contend with, and who left what to who, and people borrowing from each other, and I don't know what all else. The way it works now is if somebody needs some money they go to Miriam, and Miriam writes a check.'

'It shouldn't be that way,' said Billy. 'That's nothing against Miriam, but everybody should know exactly what they've got. That way nobody's going to feel cheated, and – believe me – you'll all make more money.'

Elinor appeared to like this idea, and asked: 'What do you need?'

'I need to see whatever you've got – papers, wills, deeds, bank statements, certificates, every bit of paper any of you can lay your hands on. First I'll have to see what belongs to each of you personally and what belongs to the mill. If it belongs to the mill, then I'll pass it along to Miriam and let *her* deal with it. This'll help her get things straightened out, too. After I know what everybody's got, I'll be able to see what we can do to make it a lot more.' Billy shrugged and laughed apologetically. 'I'm not greedy, you know. It's just that all this is in my blood. I see a balance sheet and all I can think is, how do I make those totals bigger?'

'When do you want to start?' asked Elinor.

'As soon as possible. But don't you think you'd better speak to the others first?'

'Why?' asked Elinor, certain of her position in the Caskey family. 'They're going to say yes.'

So Billy went right to work on getting the monetary affairs of the Caskey family in order. Elinor rented him a little office downtown and bought him a desk and file cabinets. He employed Frances as a secretary, not because she was efficient, but rather because she so much delighted to be in his company, even when he was silent and absorbed in his work. One by one the Caskeys came to Billy with all the documents they could find and told him everything they could remember about the family's financial dealings for as far back as they could go. Billy took notes and asked questions.

Miriam and Billy worked together. Before the real net worth of the family could be determined, all the transactions that pertained directly to the mill had to be separated from personal business. Miriam was glad to be of help in this for it would ultimately serve to clarify her own work. While her sister and husband were closeted in his office, Frances would wander about the outer room, looking at magazines and staring out the window at the kudzu-covered levee.

By April, Billy had got the family finances straightened out, and after dinner one Sunday afternoon the Caskeys all gathered on Elinor's screened porch. Even Grace, Lucille, and Tommy Lee had come in from Gavin Pond Farm for the day.

Elinor made only a brief introduction: 'Billy has been kind enough to agree to take care of us from now on. I want everybody to listen to him and do exactly what he says.'

At this, Billy stood, made a self-deprecating nod, and spoke: 'Now, I don't want anybody to think that I have jumped into all this and am trying to take over, because that's not it at all. I'm just a son-in-law accountant, and what I've tried to do is get this family's money business straight—'

'Probably for the first time ever,' interjected Sister.

'I looked over all the papers you brought me, and I tried to get everything in order. I'm taking care of everything so that nobody but me has to think about it. You have all been very patient, not getting upset because you thought maybe I was prying into your private affairs – even Grace brought me her books on Gavin Pond Farm, and I think I'll be able to help her build up her herd out there. If y'all have any questions from now on come to me with them, because I think I know about what's what.'

'You are doing so much!' cried Sister.

'You may think it's a lot,' said Billy, 'but it's not. Sister, that's the trouble. You really don't have any idea how much money you have. You want to go to New Orleans, you go to Miriam and you get two hundred and fifty dollars in cash, and that's what you call bookkeeping. I'm here today to tell you that you've all got entirely too much money to treat it like that.'

Something in Billy's tone and manner reminded the Caskeys of the Methodist preacher's sermon that morning. Billy was pointing out the errors of their financial ways, and exhorting them to tread paths of greater fiscal responsibility.

'How much *have* we got?' asked Oscar.

'Well,' said Billy, 'of course the greatest portion of the family wealth is tied up in the mill and the plants. So Miriam and I have been working closely to see if we couldn't determine exactly how much all that is worth.' He turned to Miriam, who stood up with some papers in her hand.

'I'm not gone go into details, 'cause it's not necessary,' Miriam said with characteristic bluntness. 'Most of you wouldn't understand them anyway. There are two points. First point: James had a half-interest in everything. Sister and Oscar have a quarter-interest each. That is to say, all the real money is divided up between Sister, Oscar, and James's estate. That's not a complaint on my part, that's just stating the case. Second point: The mill and the Caskey lands together are worth approximately twenty-three million dollars.' Miriam again took her seat.

'Good Lord!' cried Queenie.

No one else spoke – no one had had any idea that the value was so great. None of the Caskeys had ever considered attaching a number in dollars to the operation.

'We just wanted to give you an idea of the size,' said Miriam. 'See what I mean? Everybody was surprised. Oscar,' she said, turning to her father with a rare smile, 'even you didn't expect it to be so much, did you?'

'I sure didn't!'

'Your private fortunes are much smaller,' said Billy. 'For many years most of the personal profits have been reinvested, and not always in the strictest manner.'

Oscar blushed. 'Billy, let me say—'

'Nobody's blaming you, Oscar,' said Sister. 'You're the one who built the mill up, and if twenty-three million dollars is not enough to keep us all off the streets, then we all might as well lay down right now and give up the ghost.'

'No,' said Billy, 'it's not so much that things were unfair, they were just confused. Money was borrowed and never paid back. Money that should have gone to Sister was used to buy new machinery, and so forth. Nobody's accusing anybody of anything, and the fact is – and you all know it – that the mill could very well have folded up without Oscar doing what he did. All I've been trying to do is to separate things out again, so you all know where you stand. That's what I've done. Oscar Caskey is worth, in personal holdings and entitlements exclusive of the mill, approximately one million one hundred thousand dollars.'

Oscar whistled, and Elinor's smile was well satisfied.

'Sister Haskew is worth approximately one million three hundred thousand dollars.'

'Y'all,' cried Sister, staring around the room with an astonished eye, 'I'm gone buy me a new car *tomorrow*!'

'James Caskey,' said Billy, 'was worth approximately two million seven hundred thousand dollars, exclusive of his half-interest in the mill. And that fortune, as you know, will be divided three ways – equally – when the will is probated.'

'Lord,' cried Queenie, sitting on the glider with her grandchild in her lap, 'James has gone and made me rich as Croesus.'

'Now,' continued Billy Bronze, 'there is no reason why this family can't be a whole lot richer. You've got money now, and once you've got money, it's the easiest thing in the world to make more.'

'What for?' asked Grace. 'Who needs millions and millions of dollars? Why do we need any more money than we've already got?'

Miriam turned to her cousin with a sour face. 'So you can run out and buy your four hundred old heifers, that's why.'

'I don't want four hundred,' said Grace, unperturbed. 'My pasture's not that big. I could use about eighty – unless I cleared more land . . .'

'I'm not against making more money,' said Oscar. 'I think we should, in fact. I just don't know how to go about it. Billy, do you?'

'Yes,' said Billy, 'I think I do.'

Miriam nodded. 'Billy knows what he's talking about. If it were my decision, everybody in this room would sign over power of attorney to Billy and let him do what he wants.'

'You don't have to do that,' said Billy, a bit nervously. 'All I would like to do is make recommendations, and if you like them, then you can go through with them. That's all. Here's what I'm suggesting: Miriam and I will work together. Miriam will take care of the mill, like she's been doing – just fine – all along. And I'll take care of your personal money. If you need some cash you don't go to Miriam anymore, you come to me instead.'

'It sure would save *me* some bother,' said Miriam, 'not to have to write those damned checks all the time.'

The Caskeys all acquiesced to Billy's proposal, and after that Sunday afternoon on the screened porch, they never saw themselves in the same light again. They possessed far more money than any of them had suspected. Elinor was proud, as if she considered that her advice and support of Oscar during the hard years had made the fortunes possible. Sister was elated, for how could her husband touch her when so much money would have kept at bay someone far more dangerous and insistent than Early Haskew? Grace and Lucille were lost in dreams of pastures and herds and newly cleared land. The possibilities for the family seemed endless, but at the same time things seemed a bit vague. For the next few days, they looked about feverishly for things to spend money on. Sister bought a new car for herself, and another for Miriam. What's more, she bought Billy Bronze one, too. In her new car Sister drove Roxie, Ivey, Zaddie, and Luvadia down to Pensacola and turned them loose in one of the nicest dress shops in town, saying, 'We are not leaving this place until I have squandered five hundred dollars, and I mean it.'

On the whole, however, the Caskeys didn't spend much more than they had before. They simply became conscious of their wealth. Billy was very busy, in his office downtown. He took over the running of Queenie's household, so that she would not be embarrassed for funds while James's will was still in probate. He conferred with Grace about the building up of Gavin Pond Farm. Sister came twice a week to find out how quickly and by how much her net worth was increasing. Oscar and Miriam visited him frequently, and Billy was often closeted in deep financial discussions, particularly with his sister-in-law. Frances was enormously proud of what her husband had done – and was doing – for the family. The Caskeys urged Billy to accept a salary for his work, and he did so without demur.

This son-in-law had ushered the Caskeys into an entirely new stage of their history.

WHAT BILLY DID

During the months when the war was obviously winding down, the Caskeys changed gears. Miriam and her father decided that they should begin a reconversion to their prewar type of operation as soon as possible. Soon the military would be building no more bases, no more barracks. The Caskey mill, in the latter months of 1945, had still been filling back orders, but few new ones were coming in. Miriam had realized, from what she saw in Perdido, that things would be different after the war. Returning veterans would want new housing, for instance. Factories would have to be rebuilt or remodeled to permit new industries and establish employment for these former soldiers. The country would have to learn to deal with prosperity as it had learned to deal with impoverishment. By the beginning of 1946, the Caskey mill was running at full tilt, in all its divisions, even when there weren't orders for the lumber, poles, sashes, and boxes. Oscar had his carpenters throw up new warehouses on the property that had once been the Turk mill. When the civilian orders began to come in, as Miriam was convinced they would, the Caskeys would be ready.

When Billy Bronze took over the personal finances of the Caskeys, he took a portion of their fortunes and began to invest it in stocks that he and Miriam considered would soon rise considerably. To diversify, he bought apartment houses in Mobile for Sister, and Gulf-front property on Santa Rosa Island for Oscar, and poured Queenie and Grace's money into the development of Gavin Pond Farm. Danjo knew from his mother of James's death, and he learned from Billy of his substantial inheritance. The young man asked Billy to invest the money in America, and send him only the income. To Billy Danjo wrote: 'Really the only reason I was going to come back to Perdido at all was because I knew James was so lonesome. Now that he's dead, I'm going to stay over here. Fred doesn't want to leave, and I don't mind staying. Come see us in our castle.' Billy went along with Danjo's cover story to his mother that his not returning was a matter of problems with immigration.

The general comment among the Caskeys was that they didn't know what they had ever done without Billy.

Late in 1946, when Frances had been married to

Billy for somewhat more than a year, she discovered that she was pregnant. Or, rather, Elinor found it out through a careful series of questions regarding her daughter's times and seasons. The diagnosis was confirmed by Leo Benquith. The doctor was an old man now and had greatly curtailed his practice. He tended to the Caskeys and a few other families, but most of his patients had passed to two young new doctors in town.

'Billy will be so happy,' said Elinor as she drove her daughter home from the doctor's office.

Frances was silent.

'Aren't *you* happy, darling?'

'I don't know, Mama. Should I be?'

'Of course,' Elinor replied with a bland smile. 'Every young married woman wants to have children.'

'Not if the children are going to be deformed,' returned Frances quietly.

Elinor shot a glance at her daughter, but said nothing until they had drawn up in front of the house. Frances started to get out of the automobile, but Elinor caught her by the arm and said fiercely, '*Deformed?* Is that what you think? Is *that* what you call yourself? Is that what you call *me*?'

'Mama—'

'Is Zaddie Sapp deformed because she was born with black skin?'

'Of course not—'

'Are Grace and Lucille deformed because they have given up men and live out at Gavin Pond Farm together?'

'No, Mama, that's not—'

'That's how they were *born*, darling! Zaddie was born with black skin and Grace Caskey was born to dote on girls, and just because they're different, do you think Creola Sapp should have said, "I'm not going to give birth to this child"? Do you think Genevieve and James should have said, "We don't want a little baby if she's not going to grow up to be just like everybody else in this town"?'

At first Frances didn't answer, knowing her mother would interrupt her again. But Elinor was silent, looking straight ahead, her hands convulsively grasping the steering wheel.

'Mama,' said Frances softly, 'I wasn't thinking of *me*, I was thinking of the baby. I was thinking, "What if the *baby's* not happy?" That's all. I'd love it, I know I would.'

'You said "deformed,"' said Elinor.

'I guess that's not what I meant. I meant . . . *different*. I meant, is the baby going to be like you and me?'

Elinor glanced at her daughter once again, and now the glance was softer. 'Are you that unhappy?'

'No!' cried Frances, rocking forward. 'Mama, I'm not unhappy! How could I be unhappy, being married to Billy and still being able to live with you and

Daddy? There's not a single thing wrong with my life. Mama, we didn't even lose anybody in the war! And so many people did.'

'All right then,' said Elinor. 'Let's say you had a baby that was just like you, just like me – it would be different. And that's all. But Zaddie is different, Zaddie is black. Grace is different, Grace is never going to get married and have children of her own. But they're happy. And you're happy. Why do you think your own baby couldn't grow up happy, too?'

Frances thought about this for a moment. 'I guess it could,' she concluded. 'I guess what I really wanted to know was, *is* the baby gone be like us, Mama?'

'There's no way of telling until it's born,' said Elinor slowly. 'Then we'll know.' Elinor reached down and began to open the door of the car.

'Wait,' said Frances, impulsively placing a hand on her mother's shoulder. 'Mama,' she whispered, 'I was just worried . . . I was just thinking of the baby. I didn't mean . . .'

'I know you didn't, darling.'

When they got inside the house, Billy said, 'Why'd you sit out there in the car so long? Y'all must have been freezing!'

Frances smiled. 'We were just talking over the good news.'

'What good news?'

'I'm gone have a baby,' Frances announced.

Billy's surprise and happiness were evidenced in a grin that looked as if it might split his face, and a string of scarcely articulate protestations that this couldn't be true. Frances assured him that it was.

'Are you sure you're gone want a little baby who does nothing but cry all the time?' Frances asked.

'Our little baby can cry all she wants, so far as I'm concerned. When is it due?'

'July,' put in Elinor quickly.

'Are you going to take care of Frances?' Billy asked his mother-in-law.

Elinor nodded. Billy always said the right thing. 'Zaddie and I are. We're going to make sure that baby's healthy.'

'Mama,' said Frances, with a little uneasiness in her voice, 'I'll be fine. Dr Benquith can—'

'Zaddie and I will take care of you,' said Elinor firmly and without looking at her daughter. 'Not Leo. I nursed Frances through her arthritis—'

'You *did* cure me,' Frances admitted.

'—and I am going to see you through this, too.'

'Do you think there might be complications?' asked Billy.

'I think,' said Elinor, 'that starting tomorrow, I am going to bathe Frances just the way I used to when she was so sick.'

'In Perdido water?' asked Frances in a low voice.

*

Thereafter, as if she were a little girl again, Frances Bronze sat in the bathtub for one hour each day while her mother knelt on the floor and sponged Perdido water all over her body. While Frances never really looked forward to this ablution, she did not, after the first few times, dread it either. She actually seemed never even to think of it or remember it, until Elinor would seek her out, and say softly, 'Time to go upstairs, Frances.' Then that unvarying phrase would act as a trigger in Frances's mind; when she heard it spoken, she seemed to forget everything else. She would drop whatever she was doing, and march upstairs. Her clothing seemed to fall off her, and she would step into the bathtub. With that muddy red water being rubbed into her skin, and the odor of the river rising up around her, Frances would think there was no pleasure equal to it. After one brief stab at sending her mother away, Frances gave herself up to the intense pleasure. At the last moment, before she forgot everything else, Frances would ask herself, *Is there a transformation now?* or *There is a transformation now, but how complete is it?*, and would vow to question her mother afterward. But afterward – always more than an hour later by the clock, though she could scarcely believe the time had passed so quickly – Frances no longer recalled those questions. She remembered, in fact, only two things: her mother locking the door of the bathroom to make sure there would be no intrusion, and then standing out of the tub, with the sensation of the muddy red water flowing off her body and back into the bath. But the hour between that click of the turning key and the feel of the muddy water pouring off her was lost to Frances, and she had no more memory of it than she had of the three years she had lain in bed with her illness years before.

Billy sometimes complained of the smell of the river in his wife's hair and upon her skin. Frances, acquiescent to her husband in all else, said only, 'You'll get used to it.'

To everyone else in the family, Frances's pregnancy was another undeniable instance of the forthrightness of Billy Bronze. When he set his mind to something, he walked right in at the door and did it. When he had got it into his head to become part of the Caskey family, he had picked out a marriageable daughter, wooed her, won her, married her, and got her pregnant in order to produce more Caskeys. The family's admiration for Billy Bronze was unbounded, and much faith was put in his judgments and opinions.

Grace, for instance, was constantly seeking his approval and advice on her plans for the development of Gavin Pond Farm. With the money that had come to her from her father, Grace was anxious to buy more land. Most everyone in the family was against this, saying that Grace already owned more property than she knew what to do with over there on the other side of the Perdido River in Florida, that most of what she contemplated buying – south of her current holdings – was merely swampland, good neither as farmland or as usable forest. Yet Grace found two unexpected champions – Billy and Elinor. Billy said, 'If you have money you're not using, and aren't likely to need, then go ahead and buy that land. You'll never lose.'

Elinor said, 'I have a feeling about that swampland.'

'You've never even seen it!' cried Oscar.

'How do you know that?' Elinor returned, arching an eyebrow at her husband. Oscar said no more.

With an irrational acquisitiveness worthy of the deceased Mary-Love, Grace Caskey bought up more than sixteen thousand acres of seemingly worthless swampland directly south of Gavin Pond Farm. Though claimed over the decades by the Creek Indians, the Spanish, the French, the English, and the Americans successively, this desolate expanse of marsh and pool and cypress had never been lived on, hunted on, or even completely scouted. This land, added to Gavin Pond Farm, made Grace's holdings contiguous to the fifty thousand acres of timber owned by Oscar in that westernmost county of Florida. Outside the federal government, the Caskeys had become the largest landholders in the Florida panhandle.

Queenie, visiting her daughter and grandson at the farm, shook her head at Grace and said, 'I don't understand it at all. Why *did* you buy all that land – if that's what you can call it.'

'Ma,' protested Lucille, 'Grace didn't want us to be hemmed in.'

'Hemmed in!' cried Queenie, bouncing little Tommy Lee violently on her knee in her agitation. 'There's not anybody living within five miles of this place. You could scream your head off for years and wouldn't anybody come! And who in his right mind would try to do anything with that old swamp? Y'all are not even gone have poachers!'

'Queenie,' said Grace calmly, 'Tommy Lee has just gotten all his teeth in. Are you trying to shake them loose?'

Shortly after this, Sister received a letter from Early Haskew. She had not seen her husband since Christmas of 1943. The note read:

Dear Sister,

I am in Kitzen, Germany, working on some bridges for the Allies. I heard Queenys boy was living over here and went to see him. His wife is real sweet I guess. They live in a big castle that belonged to her daddy and it is too big for them. Castles can be real cold and cold in Europe is not what cold is in Perdido. I should be through in March and then

I am coming home. Look for me around the middle of April I guess. Ask Ivey if her Mama will give us some puppies. It sure is hard living without a dog. How is Grip?
  Love,
  Your husband Early

'Grip is dead!' Sister wailed to Ivey, as she staggered through the dining room and into the kitchen. 'Grip was chasing a car and got run over. What am I gone do?' Sister's distress was not for her dead bird dog, but rather for herself. There was no longer any pretense on Sister's part that she missed Early Haskew or that she wanted to renew her married life.

'Oh, Lord! Oh, Lord!' Sister cried, flinging herself in through the front door of Elinor's house with the crumpled letter in her hand. 'Why in the world did so many people die in the war, and Early's coming back alive!'

'Early wasn't in the fighting,' said Elinor, coming out into the hallway with a dinner napkin still in her hand.

She led Sister back into the dining room. Sister threw herself into Elinor's vacated chair at the head of the table and pushed away Elinor's plate as if it had been her own and she had lost all her appetite. Elinor went into the kitchen and brought out a glass of iced tea. Sister was now sprawled in the chair, her head down on her breast. 'I don't want *anything*!' cried Sister.

No one said anything.

Sister suddenly looked up; fevered hope was in her eyes. 'Billy!' she cried. 'Billy Bronze! You tell me what to do! You tell me how to keep Early Haskew out of Perdido!'

But in this instance Billy had no advice; he could think of no solution, could provide no help.

The weeks passed. April arrived, and every day brought Sister closer to the time of her husband's dreaded reappearance.

IVEY'S BLUE BOTTLE

Waking at dawn after yet another restless night some time during the first week in April 1947, Sister suddenly had an inspiration. It was Ivey Sapp who had been responsible for her marriage to Early in the first place, providing the spell that had captured him. Maybe Ivey could now do something about getting him out of Sister's life. Sister crept downstairs, just as Ivey and Bray were coming in the back door from Baptist Bottom.

'Go away, Bray,' said Sister. 'I got to speak to Ivey in private.'

'Yes, ma'am,' said Bray, turning around, and going back out the door.

Ivey, not in the least put off by Sister's urgency in the dim early morning light, unpinned her hat, placed it atop the bread box, and began to slip into her apron. 'What you got to say, Miz Caskey?'

'Protect me,' whispered Sister. 'Please.'

'From what?' said Ivey. Sister and Miriam had bought Ivey an electric range, but Ivey said biscuits didn't cook right in an electric oven, so every morning she still fired up the wood stove in the corner of the kitchen. She now set about this task. Sister remembered the skewered chicken heart she had once thrown into that very blaze.

'From Early.'

'Early your husband, Miz Caskey.'

'I don't want him to be, Ivey.'

Ivey shook her head in a combination of sorrow, disapproval, and confirmation, as if to say, *Isn't that something!*

'Help me,' whispered Sister.

'I think a white lady ought to make up her mind what she wants,' remarked Ivey.

'Ivey,' cried Sister. 'I wanted Early twenty-five years ago! Mama was still alive. Everything was different. I don't want him now. I don't want to go away with him. I want to stay here with you and Miriam, that's what I want.'

Ivey shook her head again, and ignited the crumpled newspaper that lay beneath the kindling that she had placed in the oven.

'Not gone be easy to get rid of Mr Early,' said Ivey doubtfully. 'Not after what we done.'

'You can do it, though,' said Sister earnestly. 'I know you can.'

'I . . . could,' agreed Ivey tentatively.
'And you will?'
'What if it hurts?' Ivey asked.
'I don't care!'

Ivey said nothing further. Sister grew impatient for more information, and said, 'Well? Are you gone help me?'

'Yes, ma'am.'

'It has to be soon,' Sister prodded. 'He could be on his way here right this very minute. He could be here before I sit down to breakfast.'

'Miz Caskey, you in my way. I'm not never gone get breakfast on the table 'less you get out of here and leave me alone.'

Sister knew that tone in the black woman's voice, so she backed out of the kitchen and returned to her bed, though not to sleep. Now that Ivey had agreed to assist her, Sister began to worry that Ivey would dally, and that the changes in her fate would not be rung in time.

An hour later, Sister and Miriam went down to breakfast together. When they had finished, Ivey dropped a small, corked blue bottle into the pocket of Sister's dress.

'When you see him coming,' said Ivey in a low voice, 'when you hear his voice, drink this.'

Sister pressed her hand against the bottle. Poison was stored in blue-glass bottles. 'What will it do?'

'Drink every drop,' was all Ivey said, and then she turned away.

Miriam had finally grown so self-confident in her identity and position at the Caskey mill that she sometimes allowed herself to fall into conversation with her mother. After all, Miriam was in close conference with her father four or five times a day, and it hardly seemed acceptable that she completely ignore her mother. Besides, more than a quarter of a century had passed since Elinor had done the unforgivable – given Miriam away in exchange for her freedom from Mary-Love. Everyone in town accepted the fact that Miriam and her mother would never be close, and the understated reconciliation of the two was looked on rather as the affection between a dog and a cat is seen: an object of curiosity, and sentimentality – and fascination. After all, one never knew at what moment the cat might claw out one of the mooning dog's eyes, or when the dog might snap up the cat in its fierce jaws.

Miriam and Elinor, however, had a common ground and interest that provided sufficient reason for a number of small private conferences. This common ground was money – the desire for the Caskeys to be even richer than they already were. Miriam would never have allowed her mother to speak to her on the subject of her manner of dress, or young men, or her conduct in regard to Sister or Queenie, but Miriam's ears prickled with interest when Elinor spoke to her of the Caskey finances. Sometimes, to everyone's surprise, Elinor and Miriam could be seen out in the yard, rocking slowly in one of the swings that hung between two of Elinor's water oaks. Miriam sat with her legs drawn up beneath her, and Elinor used one foot to keep the swing in motion; they were absorbed in deep conversation, the subject of which they would never subsequently reveal.

When Oscar called them in to supper, mother and daughter would enter the house separately, as if to deny what everyone had seen. And if Oscar in a whisper ventured to say to his daughter, 'I'm so glad you and Elinor are starting to get along,' Miriam would reply only, 'It's less trouble to speak than it is not to speak, Oscar. That's all.'

One Saturday afternoon early in April, Miriam and Elinor were sitting in the swing and quietly talking when Elinor suddenly said, 'Let me ask you, Miriam—'

'What?' said Miriam suddenly and aggressively, as if she expected her mother to open some inappropriate matter of discussion.

Elinor paused for a moment, then asked a question that Miriam certainly hadn't expected: 'How well do you know Grace and Lucille's farm?'

Miriam looked at her mother mistrustfully. She

still wasn't used to being alone with her, and had been suspecting that Elinor would eventually use this quiet time together to put one over on her. She was now instantly defensive, trying to figure out what trick might lie behind this innocent question. Miriam decided to take it quite literally, and to answer with complete truthfulness. 'I know how to get to there,' said Miriam carefully. 'And I've seen maps of the whole place. I know the house. I've been in the orchard, and one time Grace took me out to the pigpen and showed me a sow she had paid eight hundred dollars for. Once I went to see Luvadia in the little house that Escue built for her on the other side of the pond next to the graveyard there.'

'What about the swamp south of the property?'

'Well,' said Miriam, with a loud exhalation of disapproval, 'I know you encouraged her to buy it, and I know she bought it. I've seen it on a map, too, and it's enormous, four times as big as the farm itself. I know what she paid for it, and I know that it was the biggest waste of money since—'

'It wasn't a waste of money,' said Elinor quietly.

'She cain't farm it!' cried Miriam. 'She cain't do any cutting on it, 'cause there aren't any roads – and most of it is just swamp and quicksand anyway. She cain't sell hunting licenses – you know there are big cats still in that swamp? Big cats and alligators. So you tell me why it wasn't a waste of money.'

'Miriam,' said her mother, 'this is between you and me, you hear?'

Miriam didn't respond. The idea of a confidence between Elinor and herself was not appealing.

'Miriam?' Elinor prompted after a moment.

'I don't make promises like that.'

'I'm not asking for promises,' said Elinor. 'I just don't want you to say anything about what I'm going to tell you until the time is right . . . and ripe.'

'What is it, then?'

'I know that land *looks* worthless. It looks worthless on the map. It'd look worthless if you rowed down the Perdido and looked at it from the river or if you were foolish enough to go traipsing around in it. I know that. And that's why Grace was able to get it so cheap.'

'No piece of land is "cheap" when you buy that much,' Miriam pointed out. 'Grace spent nearly everything that James left her. Now she doesn't have anything to fall back on.'

'Grace didn't pay for all that land herself,' said Elinor.

Miriam gave a small start. This was news to her.

'Oscar and I put up most of the money for that property,' Elinor stated evenly.

'*Why?*' demanded Miriam, stunned.

'*Because*,' Elinor replied in the same tone of voice, 'underneath that swamp there is nothing but oil, oil, oil, and more oil.'

*

The next day, Elinor and Miriam drove out to Gavin Pond Farm. When they knocked on Grace and Lucille's door, no one answered. Miriam went around to the side of the house, and then called out, 'I see them! They're out in the pasture.'

The sun shone bright and hot in a cloudless cerulean sky. The pecan trees wore their brightest spring leaves, whole and luscious, not yet covered with summer's dust or set upon by caterpillars. And below the trees, the pasture was awash in blooming clover. Lucille sat amid the ravishing red blossoms, with three-year-old Tommy Lee and two-year-old Sammy Sapp gamboling at her side. Grace stood a few yards in front of them taking photographs. The scene was a child's palette of colors: the blue sky above, the green pecan trees in the middle, and the red clover beneath. When the wind blew it seemed that the earth was covered in a sheet of flame.

Lucille saw Elinor and Miriam and waved.

Mother and daughter went out into the pasture. Miriam allowed her photograph to be taken with her mother's arm around her waist; Miriam picked up Sammy and Elinor picked up Tommy Lee and Grace snapped another picture. Then Elinor took a photograph of Lucille, Grace, and Miriam all sitting together in the clover.

When they returned to the house, Miriam turned to Grace and said, 'Have you got those maps of that land you bought?'

'Of course,' Grace replied.

'Can Elinor and I have a look at them?'

Puzzled, Grace said yes. The maps were spread out on the dining room table, and while Grace and Lucille went into the kitchen and prepared iced tea, they heard Elinor and Miriam speaking in low voices. Lucille peeked through the door, then went back to Grace and whispered, 'They're pointing out things on the map.'

'What on earth,' said Grace, entering the dining room with a tray of glasses, 'are y'all looking at on that map?'

Miriam and Elinor looked up in one motion, and each with the same bland smile said, 'Nothing . . .'

On the drive back to Perdido with the late afternoon sun shining blindingly in their eyes, Miriam demanded of her mother, 'How do you know about that oil?'

'That's my secret with somebody else,' said Elinor.

'What does Oscar say about this?'

'I haven't told him yet,' said Elinor. 'He still thinks it was foolish to put up money for that land.'

This amazed Miriam as much as anything she'd heard yet. 'You mean you've told *me*, but not Oscar?'

Elinor nodded.

'*Why?*'

'Because,' said Elinor, 'Oscar knows everything

there is to know about trees, and he doesn't know much about anything else.'

'*I* don't know anything about oil,' Miriam pointed out.

'But you do know about making money for the family,' said Elinor, 'and that's why I came to you. If I went to Oscar, Oscar would say, "Elinor, we've got enough money as it is, and I don't know anything about oil." But if I come to you, you're going to go right out and see if you can't make some money off it. A lot of money.'

Miriam considered this as they drove through Babylon. On the highway toward Perdido, she said, 'Why should I do anything? I'm not going to make anything off it. Why should I take the trouble? All that land belongs to you and Oscar and Grace and Lucille.' This wasn't said with animosity, merely with thoughtfulness.

'No,' said Elinor. 'Grace and Lucille own a quarter of it, Oscar and I own a quarter of it, we gave a quarter to Frances and Billy, and . . .' She paused significantly.

'And?'

'And Oscar and I signed over a quarter of it to you.'

'To me?' Miriam exclaimed. 'I don't need any presents from you,' she added hastily.

'It's not meant to be a present. Oscar thinks of it like that, of course, but I made sure you got some because I knew that if you didn't have an interest in it, you wouldn't do anything about it.'

'And I wouldn't have!' said Miriam with pride in her selfishness.

'So one-quarter of that property is yours.'

'Why does everybody keep talking about it as Grace's then?'

'Because it's part of Gavin Pond Farm, that's all. And we wanted to keep the details secret.'

'Does Grace know that it's been divided up this way?'

Elinor nodded. 'She knows that Oscar and I put up most of the money. It's the same as with the will: we all have quarter-*interests*, Miriam. It's not that you own any particular four thousand acres, it's that you own a quarter of the whole – and that you get a quarter of any money that land brings in.'

'Does Grace know about the oil?'

Elinor shook her head. 'Just you and me.'

'What would Grace say if we were to send people out there to start drilling?'

'My guess,' said Elinor, 'is that Grace wouldn't like it one little bit.'

'For the time being,' said Miriam thoughtfully, 'we ought not say a word to anybody.'

Elinor smiled. 'A secret between you and me.'

'Yes,' said Miriam, with reluctance. 'I guess. I'm going to have to do a little thinking about this. Have you told Billy?'

'No. Just you.'

'Let me speak to Billy, if you don't mind. Billy could probably be of some help.'

'If you like. But please ask him not to say anything to Frances,' cautioned Elinor. 'Frances sometimes speaks when she ought not to.'

'Don't worry. Billy won't say anything.'

For the rest of the trip back to town, the two women were silent. Elinor drove with eyes half-closed against the lowering sun; Miriam was lost in concentration. She looked up in surprise when Elinor brought the car to a halt in front of her house. 'Oh, we're here already!' she said in astonishment.

Elinor started to get out of the car, but Miriam held her back with a word. 'That quarter-interest,' she said. 'The quarter-interest you and Oscar signed over to me.'

'What about it?'

'That was a gift, wasn't it?'

'Absolutely not,' said Elinor as she got out of the car.

The remainder of that evening, Miriam was lost to the world. She sat absently at her parents' table, paid no attention at all to the conversation on the upstairs porch after supper, and later could not fall asleep for thinking of the oil that lay under the swamp. She did not even hear Sister's knock on the door of her room.

The knock was repeated, and finally Miriam called out in the darkness, 'Sister?'

'Miriam,' said Sister, opening the door softly. The hallway behind her was dark, too. 'Miriam, am I waking you up?'

'No,' replied Miriam. 'What's wrong?'

'I wanted to speak to you. I couldn't sleep.' Sister came in and sat at the foot of Miriam's bed. Though only fifty-five, Sister seemed to have aged beyond those years in the past month. Her dress and hair were untidy, her air abstracted. She was worried, everyone knew, about Early's return.

'Why couldn't you sleep?' asked Miriam.

'I'm worried about Early.'

'I thought he'd already be here by now,' remarked Miriam. 'It's already the second week in April.'

'Don't say that!' cried Sister. 'I cain't hardly eat for thinking about what I'm gone do when he comes back.'

'What *are* you gone do?' asked Miriam curiously.

'I don't know!' wailed Sister. The darkness seemed to increase her woe. 'I don't know what to do! I feel like running away!'

'You'd better do it soon, then,' said Miriam matter-of-factly.

'Where would I go?'

'Where would you *like* to go?'

'I don't want to go anywhere. I don't know any-place but Perdido.'

'You've been lots of places, Sister.'

'I haven't been anywhere in ten years, it feels like.'

'Sister,' said Miriam with some impatience, 'if you don't want to live with Early, then you don't have to. I don't know what all this fuss is about. When he shows up, just tell him to go away.'

'I don't even want to see him!'

'Then *you* go away. And let's you and me just stop talking in circles about this.'

With a quick movement, Sister grabbed Miriam's ankles beneath the bedspread. '*You* deal with Early.'

'I will not,' said Miriam. 'Early is not my husband. This is none of my business.'

'Would you let him come in here and take me away?' demanded Sister, offended at her niece's indifference.

'He cain't take you away unless you decide to go with him. Besides, how do you know he still wants you? Maybe he's just coming back to ask you for a divorce.'

'No, no! I know he's not. He told me he wants to buy some bird dogs from Creola Sapp. If that's not starting up a marriage again I don't know what is. He'd have to have *me* to take care of his old damn dogs.'

'Sister,' said Miriam, 'you are cutting off my circulation.' Sister let go of Miriam's ankles, and Miriam rubbed her feet about against the sheets to restore them. 'Now listen, you are gone have to deal with Early, you are—'

Miriam never got any further with her advice, for at that moment the two women heard a car draw up before the house.

'Who in the world—' began Sister, but stopped in horror when she remembered suddenly just who *was* expected.

Trembling, she stood up from the side of the bed and went slowly to the window. Miriam got out of bed and followed her.

'Do you recognize the car?' asked Miriam. 'It's so late!'

Sister, peering through the screen, shook her head no. 'Don't turn on the light!' she cried. Miriam had crossed the room and was fumbling with the switch next to the door. 'He'll see us!'

Miriam returned to the window just as Sister jerked back. 'It's Early,' she whispered. 'Oh, Lord. Why didn't I go when the going was good?'

Miriam peered cautiously out the window. 'He's gotten so old,' she remarked.

Having removed a single small bag from the back seat of the car, Early Haskew walked up the sidewalk to the house. He was quickly lost to sight by an intervening eave.

Sister, in her agitation, paced around and around in the darkened room.

The doorbell rang twice, and they heard Early's voice call out, 'Sister! It's me!'

Sister stood stock-still and whispered, 'Go away! Go away!'

The doorbell rang like a clarion in the still, dark house.

'We're gone have to let him in,' announced Miriam, marching toward the door of the bedroom.

'No, no,' pleaded Sister, grabbing hold of Miriam's arm. Miriam wrenched free and moved out into the hall. Sister followed her, pleading inarticulately. Miriam proceeded resolutely down the stairs, and Sister stayed at the top, convulsively grasping the newel post.

Downstairs, Miriam turned on the hall and porch lights, pulled back the sheer curtains over the window in the door.

'Miriam?' said Early's muffled voice. 'That you?'

'Just a minute,' said Miriam, fumbling with the latch. She unlocked the door, then opened it. She unhooked the screen door and Early pulled it open.

'Hey, Miriam,' he said.

'Hello, Early,' replied Miriam. 'We've been expecting you.'

'Where's Sister?'

'Upstairs.'

'Early . . .' The word came as a strangled whisper from the darkened hallway at the top of the stairs.

Sister, in her near-hysteria, had forgotten the stoppered blue bottle on her bedside table. Now she turned and fled down the darkened hallway – even as she heard Early and Miriam's voices downstairs – and raced into her room. She grabbed up the bottle, pulled out the cork, and drank the contents in two or three short gulps. She had expected bitterness, but the taste was cloyingly sweet, like undiluted blackberry syrup.

She put the bottle down and wondered what would happen.

But everything was the same; she felt no different. She still heard Early's voice below, alternating with Miriam's.

Ivey was getting old. Ivey was losing her touch. The syrup had been a mere placebo, to get Sister out of Ivey's kitchen.

Despairingly, Sister shuffled out of the darkened room and went to meet her fate, in the person of Early Haskew.

She reached the top of the stairs and peered down into the darkness below. *Why hasn't Miriam turned on any lights?* she wondered.

'Sister?' called out Early. 'Sorry to—'

Sister started down the stairs into the blackness, but lowering her foot to the first stair, she realized quite suddenly that she was seeing *nothing* at all. The house was not merely dark and unlighted, she was herself blind. *That* was what Ivey had meant by 'hurting.' *Blind!* How could Ivey have . . . Sister, having already been in a state of near-panic, now opened her mouth in a soundless scream. She tried to turn, perhaps with the thought of seeking refuge once again in her room. But her legs tangled themselves together, and she was unable to retain her balance. In a jumble of nightclothes and loose hair and flailing limbs she rolled from the top of the stairs to the bottom. Before Miriam could make a move, Sister Haskew lay broken and twisted at the feet of her returned husband.

EARLY'S PROMISE

Early and Miriam lifted the unconscious form of Sister from the floor and laid her on the horsehair sofa in the front parlor. While Early stood helplessly over his wife, whom he hadn't seen since the height of the war four years before, Miriam telephoned Leo Benquith, Elinor, and Queenie. Queenie became hysterical, Elinor calmed her down, and Leo Benquith examined Sister briefly. He telephoned for an ambulance, and Sister was moved to Sacred Heart Hospital in Pensacola that very night.

Three ribs and her left leg had been broken in the fall. She had hit her head severely, but roused from unconsciousness during the ride to Pensacola. Miriam and Elinor were in a car behind the ambulance, and Early drove in his car behind them. They weren't allowed to see Sister until late the next morning. Though tightly bandaged over her chest and with her left leg raised in grotesque traction, they found her to be astonishingly and incongruously cheerful.

'Come kiss me, Miriam!' she cried. 'And tell me you forgive me.'

Miriam leaned over the pillow and kissed Sister on the cheek. 'I forgive you. But for what?'

'For being so clumsy,' Sister laughed gaily. 'For falling from the top of the stairs all the way down to the bottom.'

'It was hardly your fault,' said Elinor. 'It was dark and—'

'Was it ever!' exclaimed Sister. 'I couldn't see a damned thing! I was *blind*!' she giggled. 'But I see *fine* now.'

'You had been asleep,' Elinor went on. 'You were excited about seeing Early again.'

At the mention of his name, Early stepped forward to the foot of the bed and sheepishly waved to his wife with the hat he held in his hands.

'Hey, Early,' said Sister. 'How you doing?'

'Fine, Sister, just fine.'

'Elinor, Miriam,' Sister whispered. 'Y'all get out for a minute and let me talk to Early by myself.'

Elinor and Miriam exchanged glances. This was so unlike Sister's attitude toward her husband before her accident that they were at a loss as to what to make of it. But, nodding to Early, they left the room.

'Sister,' said Early, coming around to the head of the bed, 'I know you must be in pain—'

'I'm in *terrible* pain,' cried Sister. 'You don't *know* how much I'm suffering, Early. I am just so sorry this had to happen the minute you got back from wherever it was you were.'

'Guildford. That's in England. Bridge work.'

'Lord, you do get around. You about to go off again?'

'Nope. Thought I'd come back to Perdido and fetch you and we'd go off somewhere and start raising dogs again. Sister, you cain't imagine what it is like to go through life without a dog. I get so damned *lonely* out there building bridges and levees and I-don't-know-what-all. Cain't go carting a dog around Europe, though. They don't allow it.'

'Well, Early,' said Sister. 'Look at me in this bed.'

'I see you,' said Early, whistling.

'Do I look like I'm in shape to start feeding puppies with a nipple-bottle?'

'Only if somebody handed 'em to you.'

'Cain't bring puppies in this hospital, Early. No dogs now, and no dogs for a long time to come.'

'When they say you're gone be well again?'

Sister hesitated. 'They don't know. They don't have any idea.'

'Those bandages look tight. Can you breathe?'

'It hurts to breathe,' admitted Sister, drawing in two or three difficult breaths. After a few moments, she had apparently recovered herself. 'See, Early, what I was thinking was, it's not gone be any fun for you to hang around Perdido while I am mending my broken bones. It's not gone be any fun for you to wait on me hand and foot.'

'What happened to Ivey?'

'Ivey's still there, but Ivey has to keep that house going. She doesn't have time for me.'

'What about Miriam?'

'Oh, Early, you don't know how hard Miriam works over at that mill. You never saw anybody work harder. Besides, Miriam's not the type you want to ask to go down to the kitchen and fix a cup of coffee for you.'

'I guess not,' admitted Early. 'Why don't you hire a nurse?'

'I'm gone have to,' said Sister eagerly. 'That's just what I was thinking I was gone have to do. I'll get the hospital to recommend somebody. That nurse can stay in the spare bedroom, and take care of me all day every day. But see, with a nurse in the spare bedroom, there wouldn't be any place for you to sleep, Early.'

'I'd sleep with you!' cried Early in surprise. 'Where else would I sleep?'

Sister laughed nervously. 'You old lummox! And roll over on top of me and break all my bones again? Early, in three years, you have gotten so fat! You are as big as a house.'

'I used to work it off,' said Early quietly. 'But now

it all just sits there. But you could punch me in the belly, Sister, and I wouldn't even feel it.'

'Early, I cain't even lift my arms. What I was thinking was, why don't you go off again for a while – get a job somewhere just for the time being, go find yourself a river and build a bridge over it – and then give me a call and I'll tell you when I'm gone be all right again. And when I'm all right again, you can come pick me up.'

'That's a terrible idea,' said Early. 'What would people think if I ran off and left you in this condition?'

'Lord, Early! People in Perdido don't even remember who you are. Anyway, why do you care what they think?'

Early shrugged. He had seated his great bulk in a small wooden chair at the side of the bed. The substance of Sister's conversation was beginning to register in his brain, and he understood that she was sending him away again. Sending him away not a dozen hours after he had arrived. His jowls went slack, and a look came into his eyes that reminded Sister of the puppies he loved so much. She struggled to maintain her resolve, even as she realized that he had begun to understand what was happening to him.

Then she did what she thought she would never have the courage to do. She spoke the unadorned truth.

'Early,' she said, 'you and I aren't married anymore.'

A look of bewilderment came into his eyes. 'Did you get a divorce or something?'

Sister shook her head sadly. 'I should never have married you. It was all my fault.'

'Hey . . . Sister,' protested Early weakly, 'I love you . . .'

'I'm an old maid,' returned Sister. 'Everybody knows it. I was an old maid when I was twelve years old, and I was fighting nature when I got married to you. Then when you went away on your old war work, I became an old maid the minute you walked out the door – and being an old maid is what suits me.'

'Sister, I have no idea in the world what you are talking about.'

'It doesn't matter, Early. I just want you to go away.'

A nurse came into the room, smiled, spoke softly, and examined the bandages and the traction apparatus. Early sat very still, gazing across the bed and out the window. In those few moments of silence, all Sister's good spirits evaporated. She hadn't the stamina to prop them up indefinitely in Early's presence. At the same time, Early's solicitousness for his wife's injuries and discomforts were swamped by his realization that she wanted nothing more than to be rid of him forever. When the nurse had gone Early stood up, looked at Sister and said, 'We're still married. We're gone be married forever. You're my wife and there's not nothing gone change that. I'm gone go away now. I'm gone go build me a bridge or something, but the minute they let you up out of that bed, I'm coming to get you. You understand that? I'm coming to get you, and I'm taking you away. I can do it, Sister, because we're married and I'm your husband. So mend them bones and get your bags packed, 'cause then I'm gone drag you all over this damn country and Europe, too. You understand?'

Sister did not reply. She turned her head aside on the pillow, away from her husband. Early walked out of the room and motioned with his head for Elinor and Miriam to go back in.

Sister remained in the hospital in Pensacola. She declared that only Miriam could visit. With a dutifulness born of affection that surprised everyone, Miriam drove to Pensacola every night after she had finished at the mill and spent the night there on an army cot set up at the side of Sister's bed. She drove back to Perdido early the next morning in time for breakfast with Elinor and Oscar. She never complained of this regimen and never deviated from it. Sister was morose, Miriam said. Sister had never been so unhappy. She wasn't mending as quickly as the doctors thought she ought to.

Oscar shook his head, and carefully folded his napkin. 'Poor Sister!'

Miriam said, 'Sister doesn't *want* to get well.'

'Why on earth not?' demanded Frances.

'Because when she gets well,' explained Miriam, 'Early Haskew's gone come back to Perdido and take her away.'

'Lord!' cried Elinor, 'he can't take her away unless she wants to go.'

'You cain't talk to Sister about it,' shrugged Miriam. 'And I don't want anybody here to mention the fact that I said one word about it.'

After three weeks Sister was released from the hospital. According to the X-rays, she was as well as could be expected, though she still complained of pain, difficulty in breathing, and a lack of sensation in her left leg. The hospital had offered to recommend a nurse, but to this, Sister said, 'No, my family will take care of me. And if they won't then I'd just as soon die anyway.'

Sister was driven home in an ambulance, and Grace and Ivey, under Leo Benquith's direction, carried her upstairs and put her in bed. Leo examined her once more, told her she'd be up and about within a month, and then left. Sister said, 'He doesn't know what he's talking about. It will be six months before I can walk again. I know that. Ivey, get me a cup of coffee will you? You don't know how much I've missed your cooking. Grace, you go right next door and tell Queenie to get herself over here and keep me company. She doesn't have anything *else* to do all day, so she might as well make herself useful.'

Grace was amused. This was a new Sister. Never had she been so decisive, so opinionated, so imperious. Here she lay, in her bed with two extra mattresses and three extra pillows, giving orders and making judgments with as much ease as Mary-Love had so many years before.

Queenie was duly brought to Sister's bedside. 'It sure is nice—' she began, but was impatiently interrupted by Sister.

'Come over here and fix my pillows. I am slipping down in the bed.'

Queenie placed one fat arm behind the invalid's back, shifted her into a sitting position, and rearranged the pillows behind her. She eased Sister back down.

Sister sighed, and said, 'Just right.'

'I used to take care of my daddy when he was sick,' declared Queenie. 'I know all about sickrooms.'

'I am not sick!' cried Sister. 'I am crippled!'

Here were changes no one could have predicted. Sister returned from Pensacola an invalid, her very nature altered along with her body. A few days later Oscar approached Miriam and said, 'You were down there with her every night. Did you notice a change?'

Miriam shook her head. 'I don't understand it.'

Nobody could figure it out, but the changes were unmistakably there. Sister, who in years past had made a habit of anticipating the desires of others, now seemed to think of nothing but her own comfort. She was the axis of her household. Ivey Sapp did nothing but wait on her, bringing her endless cups of coffee and plates of cookies, which was all she liked to eat during the day, and taking her a specially prepared supper at night on a tray. And strangest of all, the only help that Sister gladly suffered was that of Queenie. Queenie sat with Sister an hour in the morning, two or three hours in the afternoon, and an hour or two in the evening. Nobody but Queenie could fix Sister's pillows to her satisfaction. Medicine was undrinkable except when Queenie held the spoon. Unless Queenie fixed the curtains, the room was either drafty or stuffy. Ivey's cooking was inedible unless Queenie was there to watch Sister eat.

Elinor shook her head, and said to Queenie, 'Sister is worse than Mary-Love ever was. I wouldn't blame you if you moved away, just so that you could get a little peace.'

'I don't mind,' returned Queenie. 'It gives me something to do now that James is gone. I feel like I'm earning my keep.'

THE SWAMP

The relationship between Elinor Caskey and her daughter Miriam had become less strained than it ever had been. Neither, it appeared, had anything more to prove to the other. If Miriam never displayed a great deal of affection toward her mother, at least she never showed any animosity. Elinor's only words against her formerly estranged daughter concerned Miriam's wardrobe, which Elinor considered embarrassingly casual for a young woman of Miriam's station in the town.

One Saturday morning early in June, after breakfast, Elinor knocked on the screen door of Miriam's house, and called out her daughter's name.

Miriam came to the door but didn't open it. 'You want to see Sister?' she asked.

'I want to see you,' said Elinor.

Miriam came warily out onto the porch.

'I came to ask if you would take a little ride with me this morning.'

'Where?'

'You'll find out.'

Miriam refused to give her mother the satisfaction of any more questions. 'Let's go,' she said, and marched down the front steps.

Mother and daughter got into Elinor's car, and drove out of town, heading south down a rarely used road that ran along the western bank of the Perdido. After ten miles or so, this road petered out altogether, and Elinor turned onto a bumpy logging track. They passed evidence of recent timber cutting.

'This is our land,' remarked Miriam conversationally. 'Oscar was out here on Thursday, I believe.'

Elinor drove on for another couple of miles, saying nothing. Then even the logging track disappeared. They were in the darkest depths of the forest. Miriam looked about, deliberately damping her curiosity and wonder, and said nothing.

'Get out,' said Elinor.

'We're in the middle of nowhere,' said Miriam, but it wasn't an argument. She got out of the car.

Elinor had already taken off into the forest, heading east. The sun had been shining murkily through hazy clouds, but in the woods little of its light reached the needle-carpeted ground because of the high canopy of pine boughs.

'I should have worn long sleeves,' muttered Miriam, following Elinor and swatting at ferocious mosquitoes that continually alighted on her arms.

The low brush recently had been burned off preparatory to logging, so walking was relatively easy. But every footstep brought up a stink of charred greenery.

After they had gone about a quarter of a mile, Miriam caught a glimpse of flowing water. 'That's the Perdido,' she said. A few steps ahead of her, Elinor nodded.

'If you had wanted to show me the Perdido,' Miriam remarked, 'you could have taken me to the top of the levee.'

Elinor did not respond.

Elinor halted above a strip of red sand and gravel, several yards wide, that had been left when the river had slightly altered its course not long before. This forlorn little beach was strewn with sticks, tufts of pine needles, and a few decaying carcasses of dead birds and rodents. A small green boat had been dragged up onto this strand, out of reach of the current.

The Perdido, a hundred feet wide here, flowed swiftly by. On the western bank of the river, where Elinor and Miriam now stood, the pine forest was uninterrupted as far downstream and upstream as could be seen. But on the opposite side of the river the land was different.

'Ah,' said Miriam, understanding at last. 'That's the swamp.'

'Yes,' said Elinor, and she stepped down onto the red, gravelly beach in the direction of the boat.

Across the river there was no real shore, only a succession of hammocks of tall grass, cypress, and palmetto. Insects swarmed in slowly roiling clouds above the hammocks. The water of the Perdido at the edge of the swamp seemed hardly to flow at all, and it changed from its usual deep red to a nearly unreflecting black.

'You're planning on taking me across?' Miriam asked uneasily, as her mother effortlessly dragged the boat toward the water.

'That swamp is going to make us all very, very rich, Miriam. You know it and I know it, but this morning at the breakfast table it occurred to me that you had never even seen it.'

'I haven't – and I'm not sure I want to.'

'Why not?' asked Elinor. She had shoved the boat into the water and only her foot, placed in the prow, kept the little craft from being carried out into the current and down to the Gulf of Mexico.

'Elinor, we're going to be eaten up over there. Look at those bugs!'

'They're blind,' said Elinor.

'What?' asked Miriam, stepping forward and gingerly getting into the boat despite her protestations.

'Hand me the paddle,' said Elinor. As Miriam obediently did as she was told, her mother further explained: 'They're mosquitoes, but they're blind. They don't bite.'

'I think,' said Miriam crossly, 'that you are making that up.'

Elinor sat down in the boat, and in another moment the current had pulled them several yards downstream. Behind the levees in town the Perdido was strong and fast-moving, but it was not as strong and fast-moving as *this*, Miriam thought uncomfortably.

But as soon as Elinor had placed the paddle into the water, the boat halted its downstream course. Its nose turned easily, and with no effort apparent in the muscles of Elinor's arms, they were headed directly across the river.

They drew nearer to the hammocks and the clouds of insects. Miriam shrank back, but said nothing. The red water of the Perdido left off in a line that seemed unnaturally abrupt, and the fetid black water of the swamp was suddenly all around the boat.

'Lord!' exclaimed Miriam. 'It stinks!'

'It smells like every swamp,' said Elinor.

It seemed to Miriam that her mother was paddling them directly into the grassy shore, and she grasped the sides of the boat, prepared for a jolt. But no jolt came. The tall grasses parted before them, their sharp-edged stalks, dry feathery flowers, and rasping seeded spikes slashing along Miriam's arms and face. A cloud of insects descended over the boat, and enveloped it like the Egyptian plague. Miriam cried out, and mosquitoes filled her mouth and nostrils. She flailed her arms madly, shook her head, then crouched down in the bottom of the boat to escape the buzzing swarm; then the cloud lifted.

Miriam looked up and around in surprise.

Elinor paddled unperturbed. 'They're only at the edge of the swamp,' she said. 'Now you have to watch out for the ones that *do* bite.' Miriam slapped one that had just bitten her on the wrist.

'I hate this,' said Miriam.

'I knew you would,' returned her mother, 'but I still thought you ought to see it.'

Miriam nodded and looked around, still uncomfortably, but with interest. The only picture she had had in her mind of the swamp south of Gavin Pond Farm had come from her knowledge of the cypress swamp between Perdido and Atmore. But this swamp was wholly unlike that: this place was vast, but cramped with clogged waterways and overgrown hammocks and what seemed entire continents of rotted tree trunks overgrown with moss. Birds screeched everywhere, and small animals scuttled secretively away. Everything stank, and everything was rotting. Parasite festered on parasite. Nothing existed that wasn't adulterated with decay. Elinor paddled quickly, and they slipped deeper into the swamp. Miriam mechanically slapped at mosquitoes and stared at everything around her.

'Elinor,' said Miriam, 'what I cain't understand, is how you find your way around in all this. You act like you are looking at a road map.'

Elinor only laughed. 'I don't know *where* I am,' she said.

'Are you gone get us out of here?' Miriam said, suddenly alarmed.

Elinor merely nodded, raised her paddle smoothly, and pushed away an alligator that rose lazily to the surface of the murky water beside the boat.

After half an hour Elinor caught the exposed roots of a toppled cypress with her paddle and dragged the boat over to a rotting hammock that looked to Miriam exactly like countless others they had passed. Orchids grew in the crotch of the overturned cypress, and snakes slithered out of a smooth hole just beneath.

'Get out,' said Elinor.

'Is it safe?'

'Just don't put your hand on anything, that's all.' Elinor held the boat steady, and Miriam gingerly climbed out onto the hammock. The ground beneath the rotting grass was slimy; she slid back, and one foot slipped into the water. She felt a stinging sensation, and when she brought it up again, she found that three leeches had attached themselves to her ankle. But before Miriam had even had a chance to cry out, Elinor leaned over, plucked them off, and crushed them in her hand till the blood flowed around her fingers.

Miriam stood, shuddering slightly, atop the hammock. 'All right,' she said, 'now what?'

'Nothing,' said Elinor. 'I just wanted to show you the spot where they drill first.'

Miriam looked down at her mother, then gazed around in a little careful circle. Swamp, slime, and decay. What had been green was turning brown, what had been brown was turning black. The sky was washed-out looking; the sun a pale white disc. The air was close, still, heavy.

Miriam suddenly felt dizzy. She looked down again at her mother. Elinor was wiping away the remains of the crushed leeches on the side of the boat. She waggled her hand in the water to cleanse it of gore.

This must have been the action of only a few seconds, but to Miriam, standing on the hammock, dizzy and numbed, those simple actions of her mother's appeared to take hours. Miriam watched Elinor's hand as it disappeared beneath the surface of the water at the side of the boat, watched Elinor's delicate wrist move back and forth, and watched as that hand withdrew from the water.

The birds' cries were overridden now by a new sound, a song that Miriam had never heard. But no, she had heard it, in her dreams; in twenty-five years of dreams, in her bed in the room that looked out to the levee.

The old song beat through her brain, and she forgot who she was, where she was, and whom she was with. She closed her eyes and listened to that song – listened intensely but for what seemed only a very few seconds. Yet when she opened her eyes again, the pale disc of the sun had traveled farther across the sky and now shone dimly through other branches of the cypress above her.

'Come down,' said Elinor. Her voice sounded muffled and far away.

Miriam slipped down the side of the hammock and climbed into the boat.

'We'd better go back now,' said Elinor. 'They're going to wonder where we are.'

Miriam made no reply, and as her mother expertly paddled the boat back toward the river by a different route from the one that they had taken before, Miriam made no remark and asked no questions. She did not even turn around.

Miriam again saw the clouds of blind mosquitoes that marked the edge of the swamp. As the boat got closer, the insects descended again and Miriam was again lacerated by the sharp grasses. The boat slipped into the red waters of the Perdido, and Miriam thought that the river had never looked so clean and wholesome before. Soon they were once again on the western bank. Elinor hopped out and pulled the boat onto the wretched little gravelly beach. She held out her hand to Miriam.

Miriam shook her head and struggled out of the boat without assistance.

They walked back to the car in silence. Elinor again was a few steps ahead of her daughter.

As they got into the car Miriam remarked: 'I thought you were gone leave me in that swamp.'

'No,' said Elinor, unperturbed by the statement. 'I just thought you ought to see it.'

'Thank you,' said Miriam, with a slight stiffness, as her mother started the engine.

One afternoon about two weeks after Elinor and Miriam's visit to the swamp, Lucille Strickland was surprised to see Miriam's car pull up before the farmhouse. With Tommy Lee following behind her, Lucille went outside to greet the visitor. 'What on earth are you doing out here?'

'Hello to you, too,' said Miriam, slamming shut the car door.

Lucille laughed. 'No, I just meant, what got you out from behind that old desk of yours?'

'I need to speak to you and Grace.'

'Grace and Escue are out in the corn. Let me go call her. Here, take Tommy Lee inside. There's a pitcher of iced tea in the refrigerator.'

'Is it sweet?' asked Miriam, grabbing Tommy Lee's hand and dragging him up the steps of the porch.

'Yes, but I'll make some for you that isn't.'

In a few minutes, the three women were seated around the dining room table. Tommy Lee was on Grace's lap. Grace was deeply sunburned from all the time she spent out in the fields. Her hair had turned a streaked, golden blond. In contrast, Lucille's face was pale, for she never went out without a broad-brimmed straw hat. She had lost her pastiness, however, and was as plump now as Queenie had been when she first arrived in Perdido. Her arms were red and freckled, and she was fearsomely proud of her calloused hands, for they showed her family how hard she worked for love of Grace and Gavin Pond Farm. An oscillating fan on highest speed was set on another chair.

Grace and Lucille looked expectantly at Miriam. Miriam had never visited on a weekday afternoon before. She had placed a clipboard of papers before her, and she took a fountain pen out of her dress pocket; she wasted no time in getting to the point.

'This is about that old swampland south of here.'

'What about it?' said Grace warily.

'First thing is,' said Miriam, 'we are buying more. I just found another parcel next to what we already have, about eighteen hundred acres. So I've bought it, and I need your signatures.'

'Miriam, Lucille and I don't have any money for more land! We're strapped as it is.'

'Queenie is lending you the money,' said Miriam firmly. 'And that's *this* paper.' She set out a second paper, and unscrewed the cap of the pen.

'Well, now,' said Grace slowly, 'nobody likes property better than me, but Miriam, are you sure we need it? I mean it's just swamp, right? Nothing but mosquitoes and alligators and quicksand, right? How much did you have to pay?'

'Eighty dollars an acre,' answered Miriam.

'Lord, God!' cried Grace, and the exertion of her surprise lifted Tommy Lee right off her lap and dropped him into Lucille's. 'I could get me Black Belt soil for eighty dollars an acre. What in the world are you thinking of, paying that kind of money?'

Miriam sighed. 'Grace, just sign. You're not out one penny. You know and I know you're never gone have to pay Queenie back. You and Lucille get one-fourth title to that property, Elinor and Oscar get one-fourth, Frances and Billy get one-fourth, and I get one-fourth. Just sign,' she repeated, holding out the pen.

'I don't understand this one single bit,' Grace murmured as she signed both documents. Lucille handed Tommy Lee back and took the pen in turn.

'Anything else?' asked Grace. 'From the look of that stack of papers, we could be here all afternoon.'

'Just one other,' said Miriam taking out a single page from the bottom.

Grace took it and looked it over. 'I don't understand this.'

'That's 'cause you cain't read it,' said Lucille. 'Grace cain't read a thing without her reading glasses. She *won't* wear 'em.'

'I see just fine out in the fields,' said Grace, signing the document. 'I hope you're not tricking us, Miriam.'

'Don't worry,' said Miriam, placing the page in front of Lucille.

'How's Frances?' Lucille asked.

'Big as a house,' said Miriam.

'What is this paper?' asked Grace.

'Permission to drill,' replied Miriam, clipping it back to the board.

'What the hell does that mean?' demanded Grace.

Miriam stood up. 'That means,' she said, 'that there is oil under all that swampland.'

'Lord!' cried Lucille, putting down Tommy Lee. 'You are joking, Miriam!'

'I am not. I am going to Houston in a couple of weeks and talk to some people.'

'You mean,' said Grace, 'that you just got me to sign a paper I couldn't even read that says some old oil company can bring in their men and their machinery and their I-don't-know-what-all and tear up our property? Is that what I just signed? Where are my reading glasses?'

'That's right,' said Miriam, heading toward the door.

'They're all gone sink in the quicksand,' said Lucille in consolation.

'Lord, Grace,' said Miriam, with her hand on the doorknob, 'they're not gone bother *you*.'

'They'll be there!'

'Two miles away, you're not even gone hear 'em.'

'How you know there's oil down there?' asked Lucille. 'You send somebody swimming down to the bottom of that old swamp?'

'Elinor said so,' Miriam said as she walked out the door.

Grace and Lucille stood together in the doorway, watching Miriam get back into her car. 'Don't you bring any more papers out here to me,' cried Grace, ''cause I'm gone tear 'em up in your face!'

Miriam switched on the ignition, turned the car around, and called out the window, 'Lucille, nine months from now, you are gone be sewing dresses out of one-hundred-dollar bills!'

TWINS

Late one morning before anyone had come home for dinner, Frances and Elinor sat on the screened porch. The day was already hot, and the kudzu leaves on the levee were wilted. Frances sat close to the edge of the porch to catch the rare gusts of air that wafted across the yard. Her mother rocked slowly on the glider, taking in the hem of an old skirt for Zaddie.

Frances was in great discomfort. Her frame was not large, and the distension of her pregnant stomach was enormous. More than anything, she longed for her old sense of balance, for a feeling of walking upright again. Now she could move across the room only with difficulty, if not actual pain.

'Mama,' sighed Frances, 'I didn't know it was gone be like this. Right now, I feel like I don't want to *move* until I go into labor.'

'I know it's hard, darling, but you've got to get up

and move around. You've got to get a little exercise, for the sake of your children.'

'Children?' repeated Frances in astonishment.

Elinor looked up as if she had spoken inadvertently. 'Yes,' she said after a moment, 'twins. Sweetheart, why in the world do you think you're so big?'

'Mama, how do you know for sure?'

'I know,' said Elinor, 'because I was a twin, too.'

'You told me you had a sister, but you never told me—'

'Nerita and I were twins, that's right. But we were even more different than you and Miriam.'

'All right, but how do you know *I'm* gone have twins?'

Elinor didn't answer at first. 'Frances,' she then said softly, 'come over here and sit beside me on the glider.'

With some careful maneuvering Frances did so. Elinor continued to rock the glider with her foot, slowly and rhythmically. Frances started to speak, but Elinor said, 'Shhh! Close your eyes, darling.' Frances obeyed.

'Block out the light. Block out the sun and the heat. Listen to me and what I say and don't think of anything else.'

Elinor spoke in a low, soft voice as she methodically stitched in the new hem on the skirt in her lap. 'Frances darling, you hear me speaking to you and you hear my voice. You feel that little breeze on the back of your neck and you know that breeze blew over the Perdido because you can smell the river in that air. You smell that water and you know where that breeze came from. You know what trees and what branches it blew through. You smell those water oaks. Water oaks have a different smell from all other trees and even from each other. Water oaks even have names the way you and I have names, only we can't say them aloud. When the wind blows through a water oak the water oak speaks its name. You hear those names?'

Frances nodded slowly.

'You keep your eyes closed and it's black behind there, it's black inside your whole body and there's Frances right inside her own body and no light will ever get in and it's like being at the bottom of the river with no light reaching you through the muddy water. But oh Lord, Frances. You can see what there is to see in there. You can go anywhere you want in that darkness, just like you could swim anywhere on the bottom of the river if you wanted to. You try it. See, you're not on the bottom after all. You can dive down deeper, so do it. Now go even deeper. You can see where you're going even though there's no light. Go all the way down. See how easy it is? Oh, Frances, you know what you're looking for. You're looking for two little babies, two little babies that are all yours. I remember, Frances, I remember going down to the bottom once and seeing you, and I thought, "Oh, this little girl is precious. I'm going to love this little girl like nobody's business," and you know what? Your eyes were open, and you looked back at me and your mouth opened, and you said, "Hey, Mama," and I said, "Hey, little girl" because you didn't have a name yet. You . . .'

Elinor broke off. Beside her, Frances's body was rigid, her eyelids were quivering, and her mouth twitched. Elinor heard a car pull up in front of the house. By its sound she knew it to be Oscar's. She went on speaking to her daughter in a voice that was much lower, quicker, and more urgent.

'See, Frances, two babies, just like I told you. See, they're just fine, both of them, so swim back on up to the top. Say goodbye to your babies – *don't touch them* – and turn around and swim back up. Go right back up to your eyelids. You'll be able to find them; they're little cracks of sunlight. Swim straight up. Hurry, darling. When you get back up there, turn around just one more time and sit down slowly and get yourself comfortable again, and now, Frances, *open your eyes.*'

Downstairs, the screen door slammed, and the hallway was filled with the voices of Elinor's husband and eldest daughter.

Frances's eyes were open and she was trembling. 'Mama—' she whispered.

'Shhh!'

Oscar was coming up the stairs.

'Mama!' cried Frances peremptorily.

Elinor turned to her daughter. 'Twins?'

'There were two of them,' answered Frances evasively.

'Two girls? Like Nerita and me?'

'One of them was a girl,' said Frances, still trembling.

'And one was a boy?' asked her mother.

Oscar appeared smiling in the door. 'That baby hasn't come *yet*?' he laughed. 'Frances, I am getting anxious for my first grandchild. You ought to hurry it up.'

'And one was a boy?' whispered Elinor anxiously in her daughter's ear.

'One of them was a girl,' Frances repeated, and awkwardly raised herself from the glider.

Frances was silent during the noontime meal that day and excused herself before anyone else was finished. She retreated to her room. Billy started to get up and follow her, but putting aside her napkin, Elinor said, 'No. You stay here, let me see about her.'

Frances lay on the bed atop the covers, dry-eyed and motionless. All the shades in the room were drawn, and it was stifling hot.

'Let me turn on the fan,' said Elinor as she entered.

She crossed the room and sat on the edge of the bed. She took Frances's limp, sweating hand in her own.

'Mama,' said Frances, 'when the time comes . . .' She choked back a sob.

Elinor nodded. 'When the time comes for you to have your babies . . .'

'. . . I want you there, and nobody else. Nobody else in the whole house. Send Billy and Daddy away. Send Zaddie out on an errand.'

'I'll need some help, darling. Zaddie can help me.'

'No, I—'

'There's nothing,' said Elinor slowly, 'that Zaddie hasn't seen and doesn't know about. Do you understand what I'm saying? There's nothing that Zaddie wouldn't do for me and you. That's been true ever since Zaddie was a little tiny girl and used to rake the yards for Mary-Love.'

Elinor continued to hold her daughter's hand.

'Mama,' whispered Frances, weeping now, 'you know what I saw?'

Elinor nodded. 'I know now. I know why you're upset.'

'Shouldn't I be!'

Elinor smiled. 'It's just like Nerita and me. Those two babies are going to be as different as night and day, as different as air and water, as different as life and death.'

'But what will I do—'

'I'll *show* you what to do, darling, there's nothing to worry about. All I have to do is think of a way to get Oscar and Billy out of the house when the time comes.'

Frances's belly continued to swell, to the point that even Billy and Oscar wondered whether she was carrying more than just one child. Frances was depressed, and asked that her husband sleep in the front room; she was too uncomfortable, she said, sharing a bed at this time. Billy complied without a murmur.

At the beginning of July, Frances began to press her mother to have Oscar and Billy leave the house. When she gave birth, she wanted to make sure that she was alone.

One morning after breakfast, the moment that Oscar and Billy had walked out of the door on their way to work, Frances said to her mother: 'One week.'

'You know for sure?' Elinor asked, pleased.

'Yes,' replied Frances. 'One week for sure.'

'Frances, it's going to be hard to get Oscar and Billy out of the house. Billy is going to want to stay here with you. Wouldn't it make more sense for you and Zaddie and me to go off somewhere for a few days?'

Frances looked at her mother strangely. 'No,' she said, with a touch of surprise in her voice. 'Mama, you know we have to be near the river.'

Elinor smiled, as if her suggestion had been a kind of test and Frances had given the right answer.

'Sweetheart,' said Elinor, 'you're changing, you know that?'

Frances nodded. Her smile was rueful. 'I know things I didn't use to know.'

'It's difficult for you . . .'

'Yes, ma'am,' agreed Frances. 'But I don't have any choice, do I?'

Elinor shook her head no. 'What do you feel?' asked her mother curiously.

Frances sat back in her chair, and thought about this for a few moments, then replied carefully, 'I feel different. I understand things I never used to understand. I see things I never saw before. Hear things I never heard before. The water oaks *do* have names, and I know what they are. I can sit here in this chair and feel that breeze through the screen and I know where it's been. I couldn't put it down on paper, but I know. I feel like there are changes in my body, and I think it's something more than having a baby. They say all women's systems change when they get pregnant, but this is something more than that. There's something different about the way I move, about the way things feel when I pick them up. I'm not sure what it is. Mama, am I really *changing*?'

'We all change. Even you. Even me.'

'Yes, but Mama, I feel – and this is going to sound

crazy – I feel like I'm getting *younger*. And that's not what you're supposed to feel when you're having babies for the first time. You're supposed to feel like you're growing up.'

'You don't feel younger, you just feel happier, that's all.'

Frances shook her head, and then asked thoughtfully, 'How old are you?'

Elinor smiled, 'I have never answered that question. Not for anybody. How old do you think I am?'

'Well, I think you're Daddy's age. And Daddy's fifty-three.'

'Is that how old I look?'

'You look like you could be fifty-three,' said Frances. 'I mean, you're beautiful, Mama, but you look like you could be fifty-three. What year were you born? Are you older than Daddy or younger?'

'I don't know. I lost my birth certificate in the flood of 1919.'

'But you must know how old you are.'

'Well, darling, some people say you shouldn't measure your age by how many birthdays you've had, but by how young you feel. And even though I'm about to have my first grandchildren, I feel very young. And you, too, you said it – you feel like you're getting younger, and I'm sure you are.'

As Elinor called Zaddie in for more coffee, Frances considered this. 'Mama,' she asked, when Zaddie had gone back to the kitchen, 'how long would I live if I lived in the water, all the time I mean?'

'Shhh!' said Elinor, with a toss of her head indicating the kitchen door.

'I thought you said Zaddie knew all our secrets.'

'Zaddie knows *some* secrets, darling, but we are not a parade with banners. And you shouldn't be asking me questions like this, not . . .'

'Not what?'

'Not at breakfast.'

'Oh,' laughed Frances. 'I'm just supposing. Now just suppose I lived at the bottom of some old river somewhere, I wonder how long I'd live. I wonder if I'd live longer than people living on the land.'

Elinor appeared uncomfortable; she toyed with her cup, turning it slowly around in its saucer.

'You might,' she said hesitantly.

'And twenty-five years old on the land is all grown-up, but maybe twenty-five years old under the water, at the bottom of some river, is not that old. Maybe there twenty-five is still just a little girl.'

'It might be,' said Elinor.

'And maybe,' Frances went on, more seriously, 'and maybe if a twenty-five-year-old woman on the land were always *thinking* about the bottom of the river, and dreaming about it and seeing it when she closed her eyes and hearing it when she put her hands over her ears, maybe then she would start to feel younger.'

'She might,' said Elinor.

'And what if – oh—' Frances broke off with the sudden exclamation and a look of surprise.

'What is it?' cried Elinor.

'I just got kicked!' Frances laughed.

'By the little girl?'

'No,' replied Frances. 'By the other one.'

Frances's labor pains began at the supper table a week to the day later. Though she wasn't finished, Miriam stood up and said, 'I'm going home. Somebody call me when it's over.' Queenie hurried away too, throwing congratulations over her shoulder. Billy ran toward the telephone to call Leo Benquith, but Frances stopped him with a sharp word.

'No!' she cried. 'Mama and Zaddie. Just Mama and Zaddie.'

'Sweetheart,' said Billy in surprise, 'you're so big, what if there's a problem?'

'Just Mama and Zaddie.' Frances was firm.

'Elinor,' said Oscar, alarmed, 'take care of Frances, get her upstairs, quick.'

'Oscar, it doesn't happen that quickly,' said Elinor calmly.

'Are you all right?' asked Frances's husband solicitously.

'Zaddie,' said Oscar, 'leave the dishes be. You take care of Frances.'

'She's all right, Mr Oscar,' replied Zaddie, and continued to clear the table.

'Or at least I will be,' said Frances, 'as soon as you two get out of here.'

'Who?' said Billy. 'Who is *you two*?'

'You and Daddy.'

'*What?*' cried Oscar.

'I don't want you around here,' said Frances.

'You make her nervous,' explained Elinor. 'I don't blame her. When I was giving birth, I certainly didn't want any men around. Men get in the way.'

'That's right,' said Frances. 'So I would be much obliged, Billy, if you and Daddy would go off somewhere.'

'Where would we go?' said Billy.

'Go out to Gavin Pond Farm and stay with Grace and Lucille for the night,' said Elinor. 'We'll call you when it's over.'

'I'm not leaving!' said Billy.

'Yes, you are,' said Frances calmly. 'And right now. Put some pajamas in a paper bag. Mama, call up Grace and tell her to turn down the bed for Billy and Daddy.'

Billy Bronze and Oscar Caskey sat in silent astonishment at the dining room table, watching as Elinor helped her daughter up the stairs.

Zaddie came in from the kitchen, and cried to the two men, 'Shoo! Shoo! We don't want y'all here!'

*

THE FORTUNE

The July night was hot and fragrant. Lowering white clouds gathered up pinpoints of light from the earth and cast them back as a diffuse gray pall over Perdido. Billy Bronze with his father-in-law on the seat beside him drove recklessly out to the farm, as if his wife were *there* and had begged him to be at her side during the delivery of their child.

'Billy,' said Oscar in mild reproof, 'you are going too fast. I don't particularly want to die tonight. Not till I've seen my first little grandchild.'

'Sorry,' said Billy, and lifted his foot from the accelerator.

They drove through Babylon. It was only nine o'clock, but many of the houses were already shut up for the night.

Oscar said, 'I tried to get Elinor to tell me whether it was gone be a boy or a girl, but she wouldn't say. She said, "You and Billy got to wait and see."'

'How would she know anyway?' asked Billy.

For a few seconds Oscar didn't answer. Then he asked a question of his own: 'How can you have been around Elinor as much as you have and not notice she knows things you and I don't?'

'Miz Caskey's smart as a whip,' agreed Billy. 'But how would she know if it were going to be a boy or a girl?'

Lucille and Grace were expecting them, alerted by a telephone call from Elinor. They stood in the doorway to the farmhouse in identical housecoats.

'Y'all get thrown out?' said Grace with a smile.

'We sure did!' cried Billy, climbing out of the car.

'I know we're disturbing you,' said Oscar with a shake of his head.

'Frances threw you out, I guess,' said Lucille, also smiling and standing aside so that the men could enter. 'About time. How any self-respecting woman could live with a man, I will *never* know.'

'Hurts my feelings,' said Billy. 'It really does.'

'I think I better call Elinor,' said Oscar, heading for the telephone.

'Don't,' said Grace. 'She told me to tell you *she'd* call. They wouldn't answer it anyway, they're all too busy to answer the telephone.'

'So we're just going to sit here until the telephone rings,' said Billy with a sigh. 'This is my first baby!'

'We are gone play cards to get your mind off things,' said Grace, leading the men into the dining room.

'I just play dominoes,' said Oscar. 'If I had thought about it I would have brought them.'

'We're gone teach you canasta,' said Lucille. 'That's what Grace and I always play. 'Course it's different with four than it is with two, but that's what rule books are for.'

The four sat down at the table, and Oscar was patiently told the rules. However, he couldn't keep his mind on the game, and after about an hour they gave up trying to play. Lucille went into the kitchen and prepared glasses of Elinor's blackberry nectar and brought it out to the dining room.

'Oscar, long as you are here,' Grace was saying, 'I might as well tell you about something.'

'What's that?'

'Miriam was out here last week with papers for me to sign.'

'I know she was.'

'Good. That's all I wanted to know. I just wanted to make sure she wasn't off rampaging on her own with all our property down there south of the farm.'

'Miriam says we're gone make a fortune off it,' remarked Billy. 'And Lord, if it can be done through hard work and sheer meanness, then Miriam is going to make us all rich.'

'I'd trust Miriam,' said Oscar, reassuring Grace. 'If she says sign something, I'd go ahead and sign it. If she says, "Write me a check," then pull out your checkbook. She knows what she's doing. Miriam doesn't care about anything but making money, and it doesn't matter to her if the money she makes goes into her account, or yours or mine or anybody else's in the family. Nothing makes Miriam happier than adding up a column of figures every day, and seeing the total get higher and higher.'

'But doesn't she talk to you about all this?' Grace asked incredulously.

'Why should she?' Oscar shrugged. 'I know just

about everything there is to know about trees, but not much about anything else. I certainly couldn't go out to Texas and talk about oil in Escambia County, Florida, but Miriam could.'

'Would they listen to a woman?' asked Lucille.

'Maybe not,' put in Billy. 'That's why she's taking me along with her. Just for insurance. I know *something* about all this — not as much as Miriam, of course — but I'll sit there just looking smart, I guess, and she can do all the talking. I'll spread out the maps on somebody's desk, and Miriam can draw the little circles.'

'My question is,' said Grace, 'how the hell does she know where to draw the little circles?'

Billy shrugged.

Oscar said: 'Elinor showed her . . .'

Lines of inquiry in the Caskey family always stopped short at Elinor.

'Y'all,' said Grace at ten o'clock, 'Lucille and I are gone have to go upstairs. You city people can lie abed until eight o'clock in the morning if you want to, but in the summertime Lucille and I have to be up at four.'

'You go on,' said Oscar, 'and thank y'all for keeping us company.'

'Did y'all bring pajamas?' asked Lucille.

'Out in the car,' said Billy.

'And y'all don't mind sharing a bed for the night?' asked Grace.

'I was hoping Elinor would have called by now,' sighed Oscar.

'Go to bed,' said Grace. 'Don't expect anything before morning.'

'I know I'm not going to be able to sleep,' said Billy. 'I'm going to be waiting to hear the phone ring.'

'Leave your door open,' said Grace, now standing on the lowermost stair with her hand atop Lucille's on the newel post.

The two women went upstairs to bed. Downstairs, Oscar and Billy heard their door being softly pulled shut. They sat for another half hour at the dining room table talking quietly, then Billy went out to the car and fetched their pajamas. They went upstairs, undressed, and got into the bed.

'I'm not gone be able to sleep either,' said Oscar. 'I cain't sleep anywhere but in my own bed. This isn't a feather mattress. I got to have a feather mattress. Elinor should have put a feather mattress in the back of the car. If I ever have to go anywhere again, I'm gone put a feather mattress in the back so I can get to sleep.'

'You really think,' said Billy softly, turning on his pillow to face his father-in-law, lying wide-eyed beside him, 'that Elinor knows whether it's gone be a boy or a girl?'

'Of course. And Frances does, too,' said Oscar. 'Billy, get up and turn on that window fan, will you? Maybe I can get to sleep if there's some air blowing over me.'

Billy did so, then turned and stood at the foot of the bed. 'Frances knows it, too?'

'I know it for a fact. Why you think they got rid of us?'

''Cause they didn't want us there.'

'That's right,' said Oscar. 'And when was the last time Frances told you to do something and wouldn't take no for an answer?'

'Never.'

'That's right.'

'What does this all mean?' asked Billy, perplexed.

'It means,' said Oscar, 'that they know something they don't want us to find out.'

Billy went around and got into the bed again. 'Yes,' he hissed, 'but what is it?'

'Billy,' said Oscar, 'are you gone keep me awake all night, talking?'

As he'd predicted, Oscar couldn't get to sleep because he wasn't sleeping on a feather mattress. Beside him in the bed, Billy Bronze didn't sleep because he was worried about his wife and anxious to know of the birth of his child. Across the hall, Lucille and Grace tossed and turned because they had both had too much coffee after dinner. On his cot at the foot of their bed, Tommy Lee Burgess tossed and turned because of the heat and the wasp that buzzed around up near the ceiling.

In Perdido, Sister sat bolt upright in bed among her pillows. The bedside light was on and she was leafing impatiently through a large stack of magazines, feverishly clipping out recipes. In the darkness at the other end of the room, Miriam sat backward in a chair. Her arms were crossed on a little wicker table and she patiently turned the knob of the radio, searching out the late-night stations.

It was the heat, the worry, the mattress, the suspense, the insects, the caffeine, and the smell of the river in the air that kept them all awake.

Hearing a sudden sharp sound, Sister's head snapped up from the magazine she was flipping through. 'What was that?'

Miriam stood up and went over to the window. She peered out through the screen, and saw the single lighted window in her parents' home.

'That was Frances,' she said. 'She's still in labor, I guess.'

'I think they ought to get Leo Benquith over there this very minute.'

'Leo's so old,' stated Miriam impassively. 'If I were having a baby, you know who'd I want to be there?'

'Who?'

'Elinor and Zaddie,' replied Miriam, sitting down again and once more turning the radio dial.

'You'll never have a baby,' said Sister with a shrug.

A single light on the vanity burned in Frances's room. Elinor lay next to her daughter on the bed holding both her hands. Frances's hair was lank and wet on the pillowcase. She stared vacantly at the ceiling. Zaddie sat in a slim mahogany rocker at the foot of the bed.

'Coming time,' remarked Zaddie.

Elinor nodded. 'Is everything ready?'

Frances twitched. The sheets were damp with her perspiration. All the covers had been pulled down and lay draped over the foot of the bed. Elinor grasped her daughter's hands more tightly. Frances began to groan, and attempted to turn over on her side. But Elinor's hold didn't allow that, and Frances began to squirm.

Zaddie stood up, ready to proffer assistance. Frances grew quiet again.

'Miss Elinor, is she gone be all right?' Zaddie asked. 'She looks bad.'

'She's worried.'

'Ever'body worries with their first.'

Elinor nodded and looked at her daughter. Frances's eyes were vacant, her mouth slack.

'I 'member Miss Frances being born,' mused Zaddie.

'You remember something else?' asked Elinor pointedly.

'Ma'am?'

'You remember what I did on the night Frances was born?'

Zaddie shook her head slowly.

'Yes, you do, Zaddie,' said Elinor. 'Don't tell me you don't.'

'Miss Elinor,' said Zaddie, 'I have grown up in this house. I have never lived anywhere else. I am gone grow old here, I guess. I have never got married. I have never had anything to do with colored men, 'cause I belong to you.'

'You're mine,' Elinor assented.

'And living in this house,' said Zaddie, 'I've seen things and I've heard things. But that don't mean I pay much attention. All I know is I belong to you, and I'm gone grow old here waiting on you and yours.'

'Good,' said Elinor. 'And you know what that means?'

'Ma'am?'

'It means you're not going to be running off tonight, no matter what happens and no matter what you see. You're—'

Frances suddenly lurched up in the bed and screamed.

With one stroke of her arm, Elinor pressed her daughter back down on the wet sheets. She lifted up

Frances's nightdress above her enormously distended and now rumbling belly.

'That's it!' hissed Zaddie. 'Here he comes.'

'*She*,' corrected Elinor, rubbing the tips of her fingers over the wet shining globe being excreted from between Frances's legs.

Frances screamed and shook, while Zaddie held both her writhing hands.

In a minute, the baby's shoulders were exposed. Elinor took it in her hands and gently helped it along. In only a little more time, the child was free. Elinor quickly severed the umbilical cord and cried, 'Here, Zaddie, take her.'

Frances continued to thrash, and Zaddie, with fearful eyes, said, 'Lord God, there's another.'

'Take the baby,' Elinor insisted.

Zaddie let go of Frances's hands. Her arms dropped like leaden weights on the bed. She thrashed no longer. Zaddie picked up a towel and took the child from Elinor.

'Turn out the light!' commanded Elinor.

Zaddie stood stock-still, holding the miry female infant in her arms. 'You cain't see a thing with the lights out!'

'Turn out the light!' Elinor repeated hastily. 'Now!'

Zaddie turned to do so, but as she was turning she glimpsed a second head emerging smoothly from Frances's quietly heaving body. It was greenish-gray, and it seemed to wobble. Zaddie saw two wide-open, perfectly round filmy eyes, and two round black holes where a nose ought to have been before her fingers touched the switch on the lamp and the room was plunged into darkness.

Clutching the newborn girl, Zaddie stood and listened. She heard a sound from the bed; it was like that of a man's boot being slowly lifted up out of a pool of mire. Next Zaddie heard a scrambling sound, followed by a hard breath or two from Elinor, then the sharp clack of scissors. In a few seconds, Elinor said, 'Turn on the light.'

Zaddie fumbled for the lamp, knocked it over in her haste, then righted it and turned the light on.

Frances lay limp, exhausted, but smiling. Elinor stood at the foot of the bed cradling the second child. A towel concealed it from Zaddie's sight.

Frances reached out to Zaddie for her little girl.

'Ten fingers,' said Elinor. 'Ten toes on your little girl.'

Zaddie, handing over the baby to Frances, stepped toward Elinor. Elinor withdrew.

'Is it alive?' Zaddie whispered.

The towel twitched and squirmed so violently that Elinor very nearly dropped it. She peeked under the flap, and laughed.

'Mama,' said Frances, 'let me see.'

Elinor glanced at Zaddie. 'Go wash the baby off,'

Elinor said to the black woman. 'In the bathroom – and close the door behind you.'

Zaddie took back the female infant and carried it into the bathroom. She flicked on the light and turned to close the door. She saw Elinor go around the bed and hold out the toweled bundle to Frances. As Zaddie pulled the door shut, she heard yet one more scream from Francis. This time it was not a cry of physical pain, but one of shock and dismay.

'No,' said Elinor sternly to her daughter. 'Don't turn your face away. Go on and look at her.'

'Her?' questioned Frances, shrinking back deeper into the damp pillows.

'Two little girls,' said Elinor quietly. 'Twins.'

'Mama, you cain't call that thing you've got—'

'Take her, darling, and hold her for a minute.'

'I cain't!'

'Yes, you can,' said Elinor, pressing the towel-wrapped bundle on Frances. A piece of the towel fell back, and Frances saw two moist flat eyes, the size of half-dollars, staring out at her. Frances, refusing to reach out her arms, simply shook her head no.

'Lord,' laughed Elinor, 'what do you think *you* looked like?'

Frances looked up in amazement. 'When I was born?'

'No, but a little later. When I took you down to the river to baptize you. Before the levee was built.'

THE FORTUNE

Elinor hugged her second granddaughter close with the happy memory. 'Zaddie followed me down there in the middle of the night because she didn't know *what* I was going to do with you. She saw me throw you in the water—'

'You threw me in the river!'

'Of course. And then Zaddie waded right out there, and she picked you up. Except you didn't look like Frances Caskey that got born that morning, you looked like *this*.'

With that Elinor pulled the towel away, and before her daughter could protest, thrust the second child into Frances's unwilling arms.

Frances grimaced and shivered and tried to hand it back, but Elinor stepped out of reach. 'You be careful,' Elinor said, 'she's slippery.'

For a moment Frances looked as if she were about to throw the thing from her, but then it made a little swollen cry, rather like that of a kitten fallen into a pail of rainwater. Instinctively, Frances pressed it to her breast. The damp-sounding mewling continued.

'What's wrong with her?' Frances asked. 'Why is she crying like this?'

'She's drowning,' said Elinor.

'Drowning?!'

'In the air. She needs to be in water.'

'Is she gone die?' Frances asked with a tremor in her voice.

Elinor shook her head. 'All I have to do is take her down to the river and throw her in. She'll be all right.'

'Who'll take care of her?'

At first Elinor didn't answer. 'She'll be all right,' is all Elinor finally said.

'Mama, are you sure?'

'I thought you didn't want her.'

'Well,' said Frances, who still held the changeling infant against her breast so she would not have to look at it directly, 'I don't want Billy to see her, or even Zaddie—' She glanced nervously at the bathroom door, as if she had forgot that Zaddie and her first little girl were on the other side of it.

'Zaddie won't come out till I tell her to,' said Elinor reassuringly.

'—but I certainly don't want her to die.'

'Look at her, darling.'

A single tear formed in the corner of Frances's eye. 'Mama, I cain't.'

'Hold her out in front of you,' said Elinor; 'and see what your little girl looks like. This is the happiest moment in a mother's life.'

Frances did so, reluctantly.

Her daughter squirmed.

'Mama,' said Frances tremorously, 'it's the ugliest thing I ever saw in my life.'

'Sweetheart!' laughed Elinor. 'One of these days

I'm going to walk up to the top of the levee and throw a hand mirror into the Perdido.'

'Why?'

'So you can see what *you* look like under the water.'

Frances returned her gaze to her second daughter, and it was with new eyes that she beheld the infant that writhed vigorously before her.

BILLY'S FAMILY

Zaddie sat for an hour with the newborn infant in the bathroom adjacent to Frances's room; she knew better than to come out before she was called. Years spent with Elinor Caskey had dampened her curiosity about things she wasn't told directly. After a long while of sitting patiently on the edge of the bathtub with the newborn infant in her lap, she at last heard a single rap on the door. She got up and opened it. Elinor, still with the towel-wrapped bundle, was moving across the room to the far side of the bed. In the middle of the bed was a large circle of gore, water, some grayish-green slime the likes of which Zaddie had never seen before, and two umbilical cords – one of them bloody and fleshy and like every other umbilical cord, and the other smooth and gray and not bloody at all.

Frances, still naked but having toweled away most of the evidence of the double birth, was seated at the vanity and brushing her hair. Her motions were weak and somewhat disjointed. She was pale and her expression was wan. But she sat straight, as if to give the impression of quickly returning strength. Zaddie carried the infant over for Frances to look at. 'See how pretty!' cried Zaddie.

Frances looked at the baby, and smiled absently.

'Zaddie,' said Elinor, 'Frances and I have to go out for a few minutes.'

'Ma'am!' cried Zaddie, in acute astonishment.

Frances stood up carefully from the vanity. 'Lord, I feel so *empty*!' she laughed, stepping to the closet and removing a light robe from it. 'I keep looking down and wondering where all of me went.'

Zaddie, remembering another time long ago, said, 'Miss Elinor, you gone be careful with this baby now?'

'That baby stays here, Zaddie.'

Zaddie appeared much relieved. She stared at the bundle in Elinor's arms and said, 'It's a terrible thing, Miss Frances, when a baby is born dead.'

The blanket in Elinor's arms twitched, but if Zaddie saw the motion, she made no sign. She had decided that the second child born of Frances Caskey had been born dead. And she thought, considering what she had seen of it emerging from Frances's straining body, that that was just as well. If it was still alive, Miss Elinor and Miss Frances couldn't do better than to throw it in the river, and Zaddie herself might just as well keep her mouth shut.

Frances slipped on a pair of sandals, and said, 'Mama, I'm ready.'

'Miss Frances!' cried Zaddie. 'You not thinking of going *out*!'

'There's no need for you to go, darling,' said Elinor. 'You can stay here. Call Billy and Oscar if you want. I'll be back long before they get here.'

'Mama,' said Frances, 'I want to go with you. After all,' she said, glancing down at the fouled bed, 'she's my little girl. My *other* little girl.'

In an attempt to ignore this conversation, Zaddie absorbed herself with the child in her arms, caressing the infant softly and crooning a little wordless tune.

'Zaddie,' said Elinor.

'Ma'am?'

'You know what to say if anybody asks, don't you?'

'I'm gone say Miss Frances had the prettiest little baby girl anybody ever did see in their life.'

'And that's all,' said Elinor.

'What else is there to say?' returned Zaddie, unperturbed.

'Nothing,' said Frances, tickling her first infant under the chin. 'Nothing else . . .'

'We're going out for a few minutes, then,' said Elinor. 'Don't answer the telephone if it rings, and don't turn on any other lights. I wouldn't be surprised if Sister wasn't watching out her window, and if she sees lights coming on all over the house, she'll probably pick up the telephone and call Oscar.'

'I put two mattress pads under here,' said Zaddie with pride, pointing at the bed. 'Not nothing got through, but if Mr Billy comes back tonight, don't y'all sleep in here. Y'all sleep somewhere else, and let me come in here tomorrow and scrub this place down. Smells like that old river in here, sure do. Miss Frances, you be careful out there. Don't trip on nothing. Sure do wish you'd stay here with me. What would people think if they knew you were traipsing around outside right after you had a little baby girl?'

'I'll be all right, Zaddie,' Frances assured her. 'Mama's gone lead me, and she'll walk real slow. I'm gone be careful, I promise.'

It was past midnight. Leaving her first infant in Zaddie's care, and taking the second from Elinor, Frances went slowly down the stairs of the darkened house. Elinor had gone first to open doors and made sure no furniture was in their path. 'I can see perfectly fine,' said Frances.

They went quietly out the back door and ceased speaking. The lights in Sister's room were burning, and they had no desire to draw her curiosity with their voices.

Under cover of the water oaks, Elinor and Frances walked slowly along the base of the levee until they came to the concrete steps behind Queenie's house. They started up the steps slowly and carefully, but Frances quickly became winded and more than once almost cried out in sharp pain. She didn't stop, however, and soon they were at the top, hidden by the thick stands of saplings that had taken root there. The Perdido flowed swiftly below; its voice and its smell in that still night were achingly familiar – and comforting – to Frances.

'Well?' said Elinor after a short time.

'Mama,' whispered Frances, peering at her daughter, whose half-dollar eyes glistened moistly, 'am I supposed to just throw her in? From way up here?'

'No,' said Elinor. 'I'll take her down and put her in.'

'You sure she'll be all right?'

'Darling,' said Elinor, caressing the infant in Frances's arms, 'do you really think I'd deliberately kill this sweet, sweet thing? See, she's not ugly to me, not ugly one little bit!' Elinor playfully poked a finger into the lipless mouth and twisted the swollen black tongue. 'Not one little bit!'

'But who'll take care of her?'

Elinor took the child, and tossed aside the towel in which she had been wrapped.

'Are there others down there?' asked Frances. 'Somebody else who'll make sure she gets enough to eat?'

Without answering, Elinor, with the help of one

sapling trunk after another, began slipping down the slope of the levee toward the river.

After a moment of indecision, Frances followed, though the pain in her groin beat with the pulse of her heart.

'What *does* she eat?' Frances whispered loudly, but still Elinor did not answer.

Frances tripped over a blackberry bush, scratching her right arm and leg.

'Frances!' cried Elinor, stopping her downward progress.

'I'm all right, Mama,' cried Frances a moment later in a strained voice. She picked herself up painfully.

When Elinor reached the base of the levee, she reached out an arm. In a moment Frances had slipped down the last few feet of levee and grabbed her mother's hand. Elinor squeezed.

'Catch your breath,' she said.

'How am I gone get back up?' sighed Frances.

'You shouldn't have come down here.'

'Mama, that's my baby.'

'I'm glad you said that,' said Elinor with pride. ''Cause she *is* yours.'

They stood on a sandbar. Crickets chirped in the kudzu vine all around them. When Frances's breath had grown even once again, Elinor took a step forward into the water. Frances, shedding her robe, held her mother's hand and followed.

'Give her to me,' said Frances.

Elinor relinquished the infant to Frances.

Together, mother and daughter walked forward into the swiftly flowing dark water.

For two hours Zaddie Sapp sat in the mahogany rocker in Frances's room holding the newborn infant. She rocked patiently, waiting for the return of Elinor and Frances and tried as best she could not to think of that second child, that other twin, the child who had been born deformed, and who was now dead. Zaddie trusted and loved Miss Elinor, and whatever Miss Elinor did was right and not to be questioned.

The telephone rang twice, but Zaddie did not answer it.

Sometime after three o'clock, Elinor and Frances returned. Both wore only robes, and their hair was tangled and wet.

'How is she doing?' whispered Frances, poking at the child in Zaddie's arms.

'She's hungry,' replied Zaddie.

'Let me have her then,' whispered Frances. She took the child from Zaddie and then lay down on the bed, opened her robe, and put the child to her breast.

'Mama,' said Frances, looking up at Elinor, who stood in the doorway brushing tangles out of her wet hair, 'maybe you ought to go and call Billy and Daddy.'

Elinor nodded, and went across the hall to telephone. In a moment Frances and Zaddie heard her talking in a low voice. 'Zaddie,' said Frances, 'Mama and I left tracks all through the house. You better see what you can do to clean them up before Billy and Daddy get back.'

'Yes, ma'am.'

'Zaddie?' said Frances.

'Ma'am?'

'Thank you.'

'You're welcome.'

Zaddie turned to go, but at the door she was stopped by one more word from Frances. The black woman turned back.

'Don't worry about the other one,' said Frances. 'She's doing fine.'

Billy and Oscar were home by four that morning, but neither of them went to sleep. Billy sat in the mahogany rocker and held his daughter, and Oscar and Elinor sat on the upstairs porch talking. Frances, wholly exhausted, slept the sleep of the dead. Queenie came over at five, announcing that she couldn't sleep and wanted to see the baby. Miriam arrived at six, saying that their voices had kept her up all night and that somebody ought to take the baby over and show her to Sister before Sister had a stroke.

Much later in the morning, Frances did take her

daughter next door and exhibited her to Sister, who cooed and made much of the infant.

'I always wanted me a baby girl,' sighed Sister. 'What are you calling this one?'

'We've decided on Lilah,' said Frances.

'I sure wish you had an extra that you could send over here to keep me company.'

At this Frances began to laugh, and Sister said, 'What, may I ask, is so funny about that?'

Frances only laughed more loudly.

Lilah was duly examined by Leo Benquith, who pronounced her fine and perfect. He deprecated Frances's decision to have the child at home – so many women were having their babies in hospitals now, and it was a good thing so far as he was concerned. Frances hadn't even called in a midwife, and *anything* might have happened.

'Mama was there,' returned Frances. 'Zaddie was there. And everything worked out fine.'

Billy Bronze noted an abrupt change in Frances after the birth of their child. In that single night – during the hours in which he had been banished from the house – she seemed to have grown up, to have come instantly into the Caskey women's legacy of imperiousness and self-sufficiency. She wasn't belligerent or demanding, of course; Frances could never be *that*. But now she knew what she wanted, and she wasn't afraid to ask for it. Previously, she had demurred to any opinion or wish contrary to her own; now she considered her own desires to be equal to anyone's. And she didn't cling as she once did. She said to Billy, 'Maybe you ought to get yourself a real secretary down at your office. It's gone be hard for me to get away every day and leave my little girl at home with Zaddie. Zaddie's got enough to do.'

Billy agreed with this, and hired a girl just out of high school who had got all A's in her typing and accounting courses. She proved to be of much greater use to Billy than Frances, whose principal worth had been in her loyalty and her readiness to attempt any task rather than in her secretarial abilities.

Billy liked this improvement at the office. He really had been in need of more efficient assistance in his job of handling the Caskey personal finances. Miriam was running more and more of the mill's business, with her father relinquishing bits of his power every day. Under Miriam's stringent management, the mill prospered as it never had before, even during the height of the war.

Miriam sought out contracts in a way that her father never had. She hired salesmen from Pensacola and Mobile to go out and solicit lumber business. She talked with major builders in the Florida and Alabama panhandles and offered them large discounts for volume orders. She had bought new improved machinery in order to speed production. She had a man who did nothing but look around the place and see that everything was being done correctly. She hired a firm of Atlanta accountants to do taxes and to advise her on how things should be done so as to minimize the mill's liability to the government. She drove out into the country and bargained with dying farmers and the widows of dead farmers for the purchase of their land. It was said that she went to more funerals than anybody else in the county. Miriam was tireless, and more and more money poured into the Caskey coffers.

Billy invested this newly made capital. After Miriam's needs at the mill were taken care of, Billy worked out schemes with bonds, stocks, and personal loans that were bewildering to family members who occasionally asked such questions as: 'Well, Billy, what have you been doing with our money lately?' He had a special telephone line put in to brokers in New Orleans, Atlanta, and New York. He kept a junior high school boy sitting against the wall in the hallway outside his office whose sole job was to take telegraph messages down to Mr Jett, who operated the Western Union franchise out of the stockroom of the Ben Franklin store.

Billy prepared envelopes with crisp new notes for every member of the family every week; he wrote checks for all the bills that came in; and once a month he prepared a typewritten account showing how much everyone was worth. This single sheet was always a source of astonishment to the Caskeys. Queenie once said to Billy, 'Why don't you ever come down hard on us for spending money the way we do? I know I don't think anything of going down to Pensacola, and *buying out* those dress shops!'

Billy laughed and replied, 'Well, Queenie, you're worth so damn much that you'd have to go down to Pensacola every day for two years and just *spend* from eight o'clock in the morning until six o'clock at night, and then maybe I'd have to say, "Hey, Queenie, ease up . . ." But not until then.'

Queenie loved hearing this. How little, in her earlier life, had she ever imagined a day when she would actually have more money than she would know how to spend.

The Caskeys all eventually learned that Miriam intended to drill for oil on the swampland below Gavin Pond Farm. Queenie and Sister agreed that it was all foolishness, that they had enough money as it was, and that Lucille and Grace and Tommy Lee might be greatly upset at having such an operation so close to their home. Grace herself had become reconciled to the idea by Lucille's pointing out, on every occasion the subject was brought up, that if there was oil under that swamp, then she and Lucille would become the richest farmers in Escambia County, Florida. They could buy ten bulls with unexceptionable pedigrees, they could clear a thousand more acres for soybeans and cotton and corn and peanuts. They could buy half a dozen tractors and put up new barns and dig out a second pond, and add an L to the farmhouse. Grace was so excited that she called Miriam up, and said, 'When are you going to get on with this business? Lucille and I cain't wait around forever for this money that's gone come to us.'

Miriam hired surveyors and geologists from the University of Texas and brought them to Perdido. They were fed at Elinor's house and then taken out to Gavin Pond Farm, where they were introduced to Grace and then let loose in the swamp with their instruments, lenses, and logbooks.

Their report was about what Miriam expected it would be: conditions in the swampland were consistent with the possibility of large reserves of oil below.

With this ammunition Miriam was prepared to take on Houston.

After Miriam had formally asked Billy to accompany her on the trip, Billy said to Frances, 'Do you mind if I go with Miriam?'

'Of course not,' said Frances. 'She may need you out there. Though that's a bit hard to imagine, knowing Miriam.'

Miriam and Billy made appointments to visit a

number of oil companies during the ten days that they were to be in Houston. Miriam planned to show them the maps and the surveyors' and the geologists' reports and then ask, in effect, 'What next?'

One hot August afternoon, while Miriam was sitting across from him in his office, Billy ventured to say to Miriam, 'Are you sure this is the way things are usually done in the oil business?'

'No,' returned Miriam, unperturbed, 'but it's the way I'm gone do it.'

'What if they laugh in your face? I mean, who's *not* going to laugh when you tell them that they ought to drill for oil in Florida? Whoever heard of oil in Florida before? Aren't they going to say, "Watch out for the alligators!"?'

'They might,' said Miriam. 'But in two years I'll be the one who's laughing.'

'How can you be so sure of yourself?' asked Billy.

'Because,' said Miriam, thoughtfully, 'when it comes down to it, I trust what Elinor says, and she says there's oil down there.'

Billy smiled and looked askance at this. One of his trousers' legs was caught in the fan beneath the desk and he reached down to free it. His cuffs were always frayed from being caught so often. When he looked up, Miriam was slowly moving about the office with a rolled-up financial journal, stalking a wasp that had flown in the window.

'How does Miz Caskey know anything about whether there's oil under that land?' Billy asked.

'How the hell should I know?' said Miriam as she deftly swatted the wasp. When it dropped dazed to the floor, she crushed it with her shoe and kicked the carcass beneath a bookcase. 'But I'm convinced she *does* and that's what matters. Elinor may have given me away when I was a baby. She may never have loved me one-tenth of how much she loves Frances. She may not even love me as much as she loves *you*, Billy. But Elinor doesn't lie to me. That's one thing I can say for her. If Elinor pulls me behind a curtain and tells me there's oil under the swamp, then I'm gone row out there with a pump in the back of my boat.'

'I think you're taking a chance,' said Billy.

'I don't care what you think,' said Miriam offhandedly. 'I just need to know if you'll go to Houston with me.'

'Of course, I'll go. I've already told you I would.'

Miriam sat down again and unrolled the journal she had swatted the wasp with. 'I wonder if we shouldn't pretend we're married and that you're the one who's really in charge.'

Billy laughed. 'Nobody would believe *that* for a minute.'

'I guess not,' said Miriam, with complacency.

SILVER

Although Frances raised no objection to Billy's going off to Texas, Sister was furious with Miriam for planning such a trip. She claimed she was being 'deserted,' left alone to the wolves and starvation, and rendered defenseless prey to thieves, rapists, and perhaps even her husband.

Miriam listened to Sister's ravings from the next room as she packed. Queenie sat at the side of Sister's bed patiently taping Sister's clipped recipes to file cards, even though she knew that these dishes would never be prepared.

When Sister's voice had finally given out and Miriam had snapped her bags shut, Miriam entered Sister's room and said, 'Queenie is gone take care of you just the same as always, Sister. And Ivey is gone sleep here at night so you won't be alone. You have a telephone on your bedside table and you can call anybody in the world to come and help you if you think you need help.'

'Say goodbye to me now, Miriam, 'cause I won't be alive when you get back,' returned Sister in a doleful voice.

Sister's accusations and predictions did not deter Miriam one inch from her long-laid plans. 'Sister,' Miriam said, 'you are getting more and more like Grandmama every day.'

'I am not!'

'I never thought I'd see it,' mused Miriam to Queenie.

Thereafter, Sister voiced no more objections to Miriam's trip to Texas.

Billy and Miriam drove off one Sunday afternoon early in September, with an appointment at the American Oil Company in Houston on Tuesday morning. The Caskeys, still in their Sunday clothes, sat on the screened porch at Elinor's and, with the fragrance of Miriam's soap still lingering in the air, said how lonesome they were already. Oscar stood and yelled out to Sister, dimly visible through the window of her bedroom next door, 'Let Bray and Queenie bring you over here, Sister.'

'It'd kill me, Oscar! At least have the decency to let me rot in peace!' Sister yelled back.

In the first few days of Miriam's absence, Sister sulked. At times she even sent Queenie away.

One evening Sister had lain alone in her room, leafing through her magazines as usual looking for recipes, clipping them out, arranging them on the bedspread into full-fledged wedding dinners, champagne breakfasts – Sister had never tasted champagne – and country brunches. She avidly read a twenty-year-old copy of Emily Post's *Etiquette*, wondering at *so* much silver to be used for a late breakfast, and so much *other* silver to be used at tea, and the number of glasses for dinner. At ten o'clock she telephoned Queenie and demanded querulously, 'What happened to all James's silver?'

'It's right here,' said Queenie. 'Nothing's happened to it.'

'Bring it over here and let me see it.'

'Lord, Sister,' cried Queenie, 'you know how much of that stuff there is! You send me a couple of wheelbarrows, and I'll send them back loaded down.'

'Bring me a case or two over here.'

Queenie didn't argue. She couldn't *begin* to think of a reason why Sister would want any of James's silver, yet obediently she went to the pantry where some of it was kept and took out two heavy mahogany boxes. One contained a sterling flatware set for twelve, engraved with a 'C.' In the other was a jumbled array of serving pieces of various design; many of them were antique, and many had been made for such an obscure purpose that Queenie was sometimes at a loss which end to pick up.

Holding the two boxes in her encircling arms,

Queenie kicked at the frame of the hooked screen door at Sister's. After a few moments Ivey was roused out of the bed that had been set up for her in the corner of the dining room. She unhooked the door, stared at Queenie, and mumbled, 'She sure is running you ragged.'

'Go back to bed,' said Queenie. 'Good-night.'

She went upstairs with the silver and laid the boxes on the side of Sister's bed.

'There's more over there, isn't there?' said Sister anxiously.

Queenie nodded. 'A lot more.'

'Good,' said Sister. 'Go home now. Go to bed. Thank you.'

Sister lay back on the pillows and listened closely to the progress of Queenie's footsteps through the house. When she heard the screen door slam shut, she sat up and greedily spilled out the contents of the boxes over her injured leg.

For an hour, Sister picked up the pieces of silver one by one, examined each for marks and initials and scratches, and then placed them carefully back in their boxes. In her mind's eye, Sister feverishly saw a large country estate – a much-improved Gavin Pond Farm, actually – and the weekend parties she would herself give. She imagined well-dressed strangers and innocent flirtations and little misunderstandings that eventually came right. She pictured champagne bottles in silver coolers and four meals a day, each on a different tablecloth with different silver, different china, different crystal, and different cut flowers. She thought of varieties of place cards and mixed drinks served by a clear blue swimming pool and children locked away under the eye of a crisp-aproned nurse. Elinor was there, looking just as she looked now, and Queenie had a little out-of-the-way corner in the second parlor. Miriam had an office that overlooked the swimming pool, and Frances and Billy lived somewhere else but they drove up every day in the biggest car anybody had ever seen. Lucille and Grace and Tommy Lee had a small cottage out on the grounds, just visible through the trees, and wore wide-brimmed sun hats and flowered dresses, and didn't show up until five o'clock when they walked around and apologized and shook hands with everybody. Among them all stood Sister herself, cool and detached and smiling, seemingly everywhere at once, greeting her guests, checking with Ivey and Zaddie and Roxie in the kitchen, telling Bray what to do about the garden now. Then she would drop elegantly into a soft chair in the corner for a few seconds to catch her breath between so many exigencies of sociability. Early Haskew was part of the picture, too. He was out by the big iron gate, grasping the bars with white-knuckled hands and aching to get in. The big cars blew their horns at him as they approached and he had to move aside to let them pass. The gates were clanged shut before he could gain entrance.

Now the last piece of silver had gone back into its box. Wondering whether she should empty them all out again and start over or whether she ought to turn out the light and try to sleep for a few hours, she looked up. Early Haskew stood framed in the doorway.

'What the hell are you doing?' he asked.

Sister closed her eyes and fell back on her pillow, praying for the barred gates to swing shut in Early's face.

She opened her eyes and Early stepped into the room.

'How did you get in here?' demanded Sister tremulously.

The lids of both boxes banged shut.

'The door was unhooked downstairs. Anybody could have gotten in,' said Early casually as he sat down. Early was nearly fifty-five years old, vast and coarse, with skin burned many times by many suns. It was brown and creased like the leather of an old boot one finds at the back of a closet. His red, watery eyes were sunk deep into his head. The teeth he had left were chipped and blackened. He brought in with him the smell of red dust, which was visible on his trouser cuffs, and the red powder had sifted over his boots. The sleeves of his shirt were rolled up over his arms, and the undershirt beneath it was grimy with sweat.

'Why'd you come here?'

'I've been living in Mobile,' returned Early. 'Didn't you know that?'

'No! How would I know that?'

'You might have read the letters I wrote. You might even have answered one or two of 'em.'

'Hard for me to write,' said Sister, 'confined as I am to this bed.'

'I came up here,' said Early, rocking contentedly, 'to see if you were well yet.'

'Do I look well? Do I look as if I have been out of this bed since the day I fell down those stairs out there?'

'You look fine to me,' said Early.

'I'm not fine,' snapped Sister. 'I'm waited on hand and foot. I've got people running in and out of here all day, waiting on me and doing my bidding. I'm trapped in this bed.'

'I bet you could walk if you tried.'

'I could not.'

'I spoke to your doctors in Pensacola. They all said you should be just fine by now.'

'What do they know?'

'They're doctors.' Early shrugged. 'They know about what doctors are supposed to know, I guess.'

Sister glanced at the clock. 'It's one o'clock in the morning. What are you doing walking in somebody's house at one o'clock in the morning?'

'Got lonesome down in Mobile, Sister. Thought I'd come up to Perdido and visit with you a spell.'

'I think you can turn around and drive right back to Mobile. I think you don't even have to stop in Mobile, but can drive on straight through as far as I'm concerned.'

Early continued to rock, and said nothing.

Sister screeched out Ivey's name, again and again. After a bit, Ivey in her vast nightdress appeared in the doorway.

'Hey, Ivey, how you?' said Early.

'Hey, Mr Early,' replied Ivey.

'Call the police,' said Sister. 'Tell them to come get this man.'

'Don't do it, Ivey,' said Early quietly.

'No, sir,' said Ivey, starting to retreat into the darkness of the hallway. 'All this not none of my business.'

'I'll get rid of you, Ivey,' Sister threatened.

'Yes, ma'am.'

Sister crossed her arms and squeezed them tight, staring at her husband.

'*I'm* gone call the police,' said Sister calmly.

'And tell them what?' said Early. 'That your husband came to visit you and walked in a door that was wide open to the world?'

Sister didn't pick up the telephone.

'Why you treat me like this?' Early asked curiously. 'Why you so mean to me, Sister? You weren't always mean. Now you acting more like your mama than anything else.'

'I'm *not* like Mama,' protested Sister, 'not a bit like her.' She began to weep. '*Mama* would never cry,' Sister maintained through her tears.

Early made no move.

'I get so lonesome,' he said. 'I miss you. I even miss my old mama. I got me a dog, but he was run down in the road. I thought I'd get me another, but then I figured he'd get run down too, so I didn't. I got plenty of money. Most people don't have any idea how much money I have. I don't spend it, though. I just put it in the bank 'cause I don't have anything I want to spend it on. I bought me a house, a little old house, and I got a woman to come in and cook for me. Oh, Sister, she's a good cook. Not as good as Ivey, but she's good. I got a little back yard and it's overrun with day lilies. Not a blade of grass, all day lilies. You ought to have seen that place in May. You never saw so much orange and yellow in your life. I don't even have to work if I don't want to. I had a bridge built down at Bayou la Batre and I ate me a mess of shrimp. Went out on one of them shrimp boats one day and sat and drank beer and ate shrimp the whole damn day. Kept thinking: "I sure do wish that when I went back home Sister'd be there. I sure do wish I had some company in the evening."'

Sister wiped her eyes on the hem of the sheet and sank lower in the bed.

'Few years from now I'm gone be sixty. Lord, that used to seem old to me. But it don't anymore. Used to wish you and I had some children, but we never did. Sometimes I think, "Sister's dead." And then I think, "No, she just don't want to see me no more." So I thought I'd come up here and ask you, "Sister, are you ever gone come back and take care of me?"'

'No,' said Sister, in a small, weary voice. 'Not on your life.'

'I could make you,' remarked Early.

'You could throw me over your shoulder, if that's what you mean,' said Sister. 'You could tie me up in the back seat of your car. You could rope me to the bedposts at your house down in Mobile. You could beat me with day lilies till I was black and blue. But no matter what you did I wouldn't raise a finger to take care of you.'

'Why not? What have you got against me?'

'Nothing,' said Sister quickly. 'I just don't want to be married.'

'What changed your mind?'

'Nothing.'

'Something.'

'When Mama died,' said Sister dreamily, distantly, 'and you were off, I changed my mind. I said to myself, "Lord, why on earth did you ever get married, Sister?" And I couldn't think of one good reason.'

'I know why,' said Early.

'Why?'

'You married me in the first place 'cause of Miss Mary-Love, so you could lord it over her that you had a husband and so you could obey me instead of her. When Miss Mary-Love was dead, you didn't need me anymore 'cause there wasn't anybody to lord it over.'

Sister had no reply to this.

'I helped you out then,' continued Early. 'You ought to be willing to help me out now.'

'Well, I'm not,' said Sister. 'I'm old and crippled.'

'You could walk if you wanted to.'

Sister shook her head. 'I'm in this bed for the rest of my life, Early.'

'I bet when nobody's around you get up and wander all over this house with the lights off so nobody can see in.'

'I don't!'

Early rose. 'Sister,' he said, 'if I ever hear of you setting one foot out of this bed – if I ever read in the newspaper that your feet have touched this floor – I'm coming up here after you. You understand me? You stay here. You stay in this room and you rot, and don't never let me hear of you putting on a pair of shoes again.'

'Early, open that closet door.'

'Why?'

'Just do it.'

Early opened the closet door. On the inside, hung in pocketed mats, were two dozen pairs of Sister's shoes.

'See those shoe bags?' said Sister, pointing.

Early nodded.

'Take 'em away,' commanded Sister. ''Cause I'm sure never gone wear 'em again.'

Early lifted the shoe bags from their hooks and laid them out on the floor. Some of the shoes were jarred from their pockets but Early carefully replaced them. Then he rolled up the bags, shoved them under his arm, and walked out the door.

'Ivey! Ivey!' Sister screamed. 'Lock that door behind him!'

NERITA

'Elinor,' said Oscar, as he climbed into bed one night shortly after Miriam and Billy had left for Texas, 'our baby is grieving.'

'Frances?'

'She is pining for her husband, I believe.'

'Probably,' said Elinor thoughtfully.

'Haven't you noticed it? She is off in another world sometimes.'

'I have noticed,' admitted Elinor, slipping into bed beside Oscar.

'Do you think you should speak to her?'

'And say what?' asked Elinor.

'Oh,' said Oscar vaguely, 'you could tell her that Billy is coming back.'

'She knows *that*.'

'You don't think she imagines . . .'

'Imagines what, Oscar?'

'Imagines that Billy and Miriam are carrying on or anything.'

Elinor slapped the back of her hand across her husband's chest. 'Oscar!' she protested. 'What a thing to say!'

'You never know what a wife might start to think when her husband drives off to Texas with another woman.'

'We're talking about *Billy*. And *Miriam*, of all people.'

'I know, I know,' Oscar conceded. 'And I'm not talking about them. I'm talking about what Frances might be thinking. That's all. You want to speak to her tomorrow?'

'I'll speak to her,' said Elinor. 'Now go to sleep. And in the morning tell me *where* you get your ideas.'

Next morning, after Oscar had gone off to work, Elinor and Frances sat on the upstairs porch while Frances nursed her infant daughter. Elinor was embroidering small pillowcases for Lilah's basinet. She said to Frances, 'Oscar thinks you're blue.'

'I am blue.' Frances smiled wanly.

'About Billy being gone, I guess.'

Slowly Frances shook her head.

Elinor looked up, puzzled. 'About what, then? Something in particular? I know after I had Miriam – and after I had you – I had low periods, too. Maybe all women—'

'No, Mama,' said Frances. 'You know what it is? I've been thinking about . . .' She paused, leaned forward with the child against her breast, and whispered, '. . . *my other little girl.*'

Elinor dropped her sewing onto her lap in surprise.

'Mama,' said Frances, 'that poor little baby doesn't even have a name!'

'Let's give her one, then.'

'You mean we can?'

'Why not? You don't always want to be referring to her as "my other little girl," do you?'

'I've already thought of a name,' said Frances sheepishly.

'What?'

'In my mind I call her Nerita, 'cause that's what you said *your* sister was named.'

'Shhh! Nobody but you even knows I *have* a sister.'

'But is Nerita all right? For a name, I mean.'

'That's very sweet. And it's just fine. You know what it means? It means, *of the water.*'

'That's my little girl.'

Elinor took up her sewing. 'Do you think about Nerita?'

Frances nodded. 'All the time.'

'When she was born, you couldn't even stand to look at her.'

'I know. But she's still my little baby girl. I keep wondering if she's all right.'

Elinor said nothing for a moment, and then quietly suggested, 'Why don't you go find out?'

Lilah turned away her mouth from her mother's breast and Frances gently wiped the tiny lips with a fresh diaper folded over her shoulder.

'Could I, Mama?'

'I don't see why not.'

'How would I find her?'

Elinor smiled. 'Just go in the water. You'll find each other.'

'I'm worried that she's not getting enough to eat down there. Leaving Nerita in the river that night was just like putting Lilah here down on the kitchen floor and expecting her to fend for herself. Can you see Lilah here mixing biscuits or breading chicken?'

Elinor laughed. 'But Lilah and Nerita are different. Nerita wouldn't eat biscuits and breaded chicken if you put them on the end of a fishing hook.' Frances shuddered.

'Mama, don't even say a thing like that! Don't you think I've thought about what would happen if Nerita saw a worm dangling on a fisherman's hook down there?'

Elinor shook her head, and stood up. 'Not going to happen. Now give Lilah to me and let me put her to sleep. You get into some other clothes and visit Nerita. Go around through the woods to the river. We don't want Queenie and the rest of them seeing you go off toward the water.'

Elinor took Lilah while her daughter quickly undressed and slipped into a loose robe.

Frances smiled nervously at Zaddie as she went through the kitchen and out the back door. She slipped through the water oaks and into the forest to the west of the house. Soon she found herself on the clay-covered bank of the Perdido where the levee ended. She stood for several minutes on the edge of the water, at once anxious to avoid Nerita and yet fearful of not finding her. She remembered what the infant looked like, with what horror that form and visage had filled her, how alien Nerita had felt when she had held her in her arms. And now, actually to seek that embrace again, to enter the water and perhaps be surprised by Nerita flinging her small smooth arms around her neck or pressing her wide-eyed visage against Frances's own! Frances dropped her robe and slowly waded into the river. She hesitated again when the water was no higher than her knees.

She felt the river water rushing against her legs and soon they felt rubbery. She knew that if she did not go farther in she would topple over. So she lifted one leg and then the other and then the first again, and realized that she was undergoing the transformation that remained – after all these years – so mysterious a thing to her. She lifted a foot clear of the water, and saw that the flesh of her leg below the knee had turned gray and thick and smooth. Her foot was wide and splayed and webbed.

Her first instinct was to throw herself completely into the river and allow the transformation to complete itself, as always before, without her actually being aware of it. But this time, Frances decided it would be different. Inhaling deeply, Frances Caskey waded slowly into the Perdido.

As the water rose, so did the transformation. She stopped every few seconds to review the progress of the alteration; how thick she was growing below the waist, what the sensation was when she rubbed her legs together, what happened if she put one hand beneath the water and held it there.

That hand became wide and splayed and webbed, as big as a paper fan stuck in the pews at church.

She waded into deeper water. She could *feel* the strength that was gathering in her belly. She felt pangs of hunger for things that normally would have disgusted and revulsed her: living fish and shellfish swallowed whole, decaying animal carcasses, children's limbs, organic detritus.

She waded in up to her neck. She no longer had any difficulty maintaining her balance against the rushing water. She felt herself vast and strong and transformed below the surface. Her head, atop the huge body, felt absurdly small.

Just then she felt something slide against her webbed hand. Next the something nibbled at one finger, and then began moving up her arm toward her breast.

'Nerita!' Frances Caskey cried aloud, and ducked her head under the water. For a few seconds Frances's human eyes remained unchanged, and through the red Perdido water she saw Nerita's blurry form – already so much bigger! – making its way up along her arm. Even in her mother's heart, something was repelled by the aspect of such a daughter as that.

Then Frances's eyes were altered, and she saw Nerita clearly. No longer was the form repulsive. Nerita clasped her mother about her neck and lovingly pressed her entire head inside her mother's mouth.

Some part of Frances's brain was surprised by this, but another part told how to caress that tender head lovingly with her own swollen black tongue.

At the dinner table that day, Oscar and Queenie were surprised to find Frances absent.

'Where is she?' Oscar asked.

'You were right about her low spirits,' said Elinor. 'So I sent her off for the day. I'm taking care of Lilah.'

'Where did she go?' asked Queenie. 'All the cars are still here.'

Elinor smiled and shrugged and said she couldn't make anything of it either.

After the meal Elinor made excuses to Queenie, and Queenie went home, a little puzzled. She had the indistinct feeling that something was up over at Elinor's, and that it had to do with Frances and where Frances had gone. Queenie no longer wheedled information, and she reckoned that she would eventually find out what was going on if only she were patient.

Frances returned to the house late that afternoon, slipping in through the kitchen past the deliberately unobservant Zaddie. She ran upstairs, leaving damp muddy footprints all the way up the steps.

Elinor was in her bedroom, rearranging Oscar's closet.

Frances burst in.

Elinor laughed, 'I guess you found her.'

'She found me! And we had the best time! Lord, she grows quick! Mama, you ought to see what that child can do!'

'You don't know it, Frances, but I have been keeping my eye on Nerita.'

'And I have been so worried. Why didn't you tell me!'

'Because I wanted to see if you were going to look after her yourself.'

Frances shook her head. 'That child doesn't *need* us, Mama. She can take care of herself.'

'Well, I know that,' said Elinor. 'But that doesn't

mean she won't benefit from a visit from her mama and her grandmama now and then.'

Frances, still excited, cried, 'Oh, Mama, when can I go back?'

Elinor laughed. 'Not today. Look at your skin, you are all puckered up. And you are covered with Perdido mud. Oscar is coming home in half an hour. We've got to get you cleaned up. We've also got to make up a story about where you went and what you did. Queenie already noticed that you didn't go off in a car.'

Frances waved this away. 'Oh, I don't care *what* they think.'

Elinor was suddenly serious. '*Yes you do care.*'

Abruptly Frances was still.

'Good,' said Elinor. 'Calm down a little. You can tell me all about it, while we get you washed.'

Zaddie, who now knew better than ever not to ask questions, mopped up Frances's muddy tracks. In Frances's bathroom, Elinor bathed her daughter and washed her hair, while Frances excitedly told what it was like to be with her daughter beneath the surface of the Perdido.

'You know what's different about this time, don't you?' asked Elinor as she poured a basin of water over Frances's soapy hair.

'Everything was different!'

'No,' said Elinor. 'The most important difference is that you remember everything that happened. You remembered *exactly* what it was like.'

'Mama, I told you, that's because I took the change gradual. I waded into the water, I didn't just dive in the way I usually do. And this time I was *expecting* the change, that's all. That's why I remembered.'

'You *wanted* the change.'

'I did,' admitted Frances. 'For the first time, I guess. I guess I didn't think Nerita would be able to find me unless I . . .'

'Yes?' prompted Elinor.

'Unless I . . . looked like her,' Frances said in a low voice.

Elinor smiled and wiped some soap off her daughter's face.

'You were gone so long,' said Elinor indulgently. 'I didn't know what had happened to you.'

'You're weren't *really* worried, though?'

Elinor shook her head. 'Not one bit.'

'Do you know that Nerita can already *talk*?'

'No, she can't.'

'She *can*, Mama. I can understand every word she says.'

'That's different,' said Elinor. 'You can understand her, but she can't talk. And neither can you, down there. But Nerita can understand you, too. You don't have to talk.'

'Mama,' said Frances after a few moments of consideration, 'can we go down there together sometime and visit Nerita – both of us?'

'Maybe. But wouldn't you be upset?'

'About what?'

'Well,' said Elinor, 'you've never seen *me* down there.'

'I know,' said Frances quietly. 'And I'd like to – so can we do it?'

Elinor laughed softly. 'You sound like you're five years old again: "Mama, can I do this? Mama, can I do that?" Well, yes, if we can find somebody to take care of Lilah. Aren't you forgetting about Lilah?'

'A little,' said Frances sheepishly. 'But Lilah and Nerita are so different!'

'Yes,' Elinor assented with a smile.

'But now that I can remember what happens, I know what it's like under the water. See, before,' Frances said excitedly, 'I'd go through the change and then come back and I wouldn't remember any of it. I had the feeling it was really awful, and I didn't know why I was doing it and it was all really horrible. Like the time out at Lake Pinchona when I—'

'When you ran into Travis Gann,' said Elinor placidly.

'Yes,' said Frances. 'But that's not really what it's like most of the time. I was so mad at Travis Gann because of what he had done to Lucille. But today I wasn't mad at all, I was just having a good time with Nerita. Mama, that child—'

'You really do love her after all, don't you, baby?'

'Oh, Mama, I sure do! You know she can put her entire head inside my mouth!'

There was a little knock at the bathroom door and Zaddie's voice came timidly through: 'Miss Frances?'

'What is it, Zaddie?' Elinor asked.

'Your baby's crying out here. I think she's hungry.'

'Well, Mama,' said Frances with a resigned sigh as she stepped out of the bathtub, 'go on and bring her in. I guess I'll feed her before Daddy gets home.'

Gathered for supper that night, the Caskeys wondered at the alteration in yet another family member – this time in Frances. It was a marked change not only from the despondency she had apparently felt since Billy had left on his trip, but from the general malaise of spirit that she had exhibited from the beginning of her pregnancy almost a year before. In fact, no one who saw her at table that night and listened to her voluble chatter and witnessed her grinning at nothing and eating an enormous plateful of food could remember a Frances to match this one. 'You must have bought out a store this afternoon!' exclaimed Queenie, to whom buying things was the pinnacle of happiness.

'Didn't spend a penny,' laughed Frances. 'Spent the whole afternoon with my baby.'

'I thought you went out!' said Oscar.

Frances just laughed and shook her head.

And the wonderment of the family continued, because after that Frances left *every* afternoon, leaving Lilah napping in her basinet. No one knew where she went. No one saw her leave the house. No cars were taken. Elinor said only, 'Frances can't stay cooped up all day. I imagine she goes for walks in the woods.'

Zaddie, who ought to have known *something*, said only, 'I got enough to do around this house without tying a string to Miss Frances's belt.'

Frances appeared deliriously happy these days. She seemed to miss her husband not at all, nor did she appear to be in the least disappointed when Miriam telephoned saying that she and Billy would be gone for another three days in order to visit Tulsa, as well. Lilah was a fretful baby and Frances seemed impatient with her, nursing her only when the child's cries grew troublesome or her own breasts became heavy with milk. She otherwise took little notice of her little girl. Frances seemed quite happy to turn Lilah over to anyone who wanted to pet the baby, whether it was Zaddie or Elinor or Queenie.

'I think,' said Queenie confidentially to Elinor, 'that being without Billy has driven Frances crazy. I have *never* seen her act this way before. And I have known her since she was a baby in her crib.'

Elinor defended her daughter, making excuses for her near neglect of Lilah, saying, 'Frances is just being sweet to me. She knows how much I love this little girl. I have already asked Frances to give her up to me, but Frances says I have to get Billy's permission before she'd sign any deed.'

Getting into bed a week and a half after his remarks to his wife about Frances's sad mood, Oscar ventured to complain that Frances's high spirits were getting on his nerves, Elinor punched his arm with her fist: 'Oscar Caskey, ten days ago you were complaining to me that Frances was so low. Can't you make up your mind? Can't you be satisfied? Isn't it enough that your little girl has found happiness?'

'What *I* don't understand is,' said Oscar, 'where is she finding it?'

THE PRODIGAL

Oscar Caskey greatly missed his daughter Miriam during the time that she was away in Texas attempting to lure the oil companies to the swamp south of Gavin Pond Farm. He discovered, in her absence, how responsible she was for the day-to-day running of the mill, and how much of the weight of the business she had taken from his shoulders. The plethora of small- and medium-weight decisions he was being forced to make was staggering, and he wondered how Miriam did it all. This recognition of his daughter's abilities and energy made him feel even older and more tired than he actually was at the end of each day; he understood now that Miriam was not simply an assistant to him. His daughter worked in the mill office so that he could spend mornings either in the forests or in the yard and his afternoons at home on the upstairs porch. It became clear that Miriam was now responsible for the success of the Caskey mills;

Oscar was the assistant, the appendage, the helper operating at Miriam's convenience.

This revelation did not embitter Oscar. It only made him all the more anxious for Miriam's return.

Early one morning when Miriam and Billy had been gone a little over two weeks, the telephone rang. Oscar jumped out of bed and answered it, certain it was Miriam.

'Oscar,' Miriam said, 'Billy and I are starting home in two minutes.'

'Oh, that's wonderful,' sighed Oscar, 'when do you think you'll get here?'

'Maybe tomorrow.'

'How'd it all go?'

'Tell you when we get there. I'm not going to say anything important over the telephone. Goodbye.'

'Goodbye, sweetness. We all miss you.'

Oscar went downstairs. 'She's on her way,' he said.

Elinor immediately telephoned both Queenie and Sister; the information was a great relief to everyone.

Billy Bronze, on the drive home, thought about how successful the trip had been. While he had gladly agreed to accompany Miriam, he had been certain that she had been going about the matter in an entirely incorrect manner. One did not simply show up at the corporate headquarters of an oil company with surveyors' maps and geologists' reports. Somehow – and

Billy wasn't quite sure how – the oil companies discovered potential oil-bearing property, and came to you. When Billy ventured, on the way to Houston, to tell this to Miriam, she replied, 'Of course that's how it's done, normally. I know that. But I'm doing it differently.'

They had stopped for a day in New Orleans. They had eaten lunch in a fine restaurant owned by the father of one of Miriam's former roommates at Sacred Heart, and after the meal Miriam had gone to the most expensive dress shop in town and bought eight hundred dollars' worth of new clothes. Billy sat in the shop in amazement as Miriam tried and bought one outfit after another. Miriam purchased clothes with all the excitement with which a vegetarian mother purchases red meat for her carnivorous family, and Billy couldn't understand why she did it. When they reached Houston, he learned.

They had been unceremoniously directed to the offices of an assistant manager for development for one of the major oil companies. Despite the obvious brush-off from the main office, Miriam waltzed in with her maps and her surveys and her reports under her arm. Her hair had been done at the hotel that morning, she was lushly perfumed, and she wore the first of her new outfits. She smiled as Billy had never seen her smile before. To the assistant manager she self-depreciatingly laughed at her inability to interpret any of this business for herself, and could he please help her? She introduced Billy as her brother-in-law who didn't know any more about it all than she did; he was just along to protect her in the big city.

Knowing Miriam, Billy was shocked that the man did not immediately see through her guile, but he did not. He was charmed, and saw before him only a soft, pretty young woman, helplessly ignorant of business and the proper way of doing things. Billy sat uncomfortably through this imposture. The assistant manager looked through the documents cursorily at first, then with increasing interest. He asked a few questions about the property south of Gavin Pond Farm, and five times he had to be told that yes, it was in Florida. He took up the report and the maps and said, 'I'll be back in just a few minutes.' He was back in twenty. Not once in that absence, even with Billy and Miriam alone in the office, did Miriam drop her role, or speak one word out of her assumed character.

The assistant manager returned with a superior – *two steps above*, Billy conjectured. The superior smiled at Miriam, who beamed back and said, 'Pleased to meet you. Will you please tell me the truth? Have Mr Bronze and I been making fools of ourselves, coming here like this?'

The superior assured Miriam that they had not made fools of themselves, and that he would have been pleased to see them even if they had not brought such interesting papers along with them. The man wanted to know if they could possibly leave the maps and the reports with him for a few days. Miriam, who had carefully seen to the preparation of ten sets of the documents, hesitated, and then replied, 'Well, if y'all promise me y'all will be real careful with them, and not get them mixed up with anybody else's.'

The man promised.

Miriam gave him a calling card with her office telephone number written on it in a feminine script in violet ink on the reverse. 'Billy,' she said, 'you give him one of yours, too.'

Billy did so, but scarcely trusted himself to speak for fear he would laugh.

'We just had them made up last week,' said Miriam engagingly. 'Aren't they adorable! Mama told me nobody would take us seriously unless we had calling cards.'

The man promised to telephone soon. After shaking Miriam's limp hand and Billy's sweating one, he hurried off with the maps and reports clutched tightly in his hand.

Billy did not realize until they had left the office that his shirt was wet through with perspiration.

'Hell,' he whispered to Miriam as they were going past the secretary's desk.

'Shhh!' whispered Miriam, and to the secretary, said, 'Bye-bye, honey.'

In the hallway, elevator, and lobby Miriam maintained her assumed identity, but once out on the street, crowded with businessmen and secretaries on their way to lunch, exploded, 'Oh, Lord, Billy, get me back to the hotel and *out of this damned dress.*'

The oil company visits were accomplished with a precision and similarity that astonished Billy. Every morning Miriam wore a different outfit. Every morning they were admitted to the office of a man on the low end of the corporate echelon dealing with development. Every morning they were subsequently introduced to his superior, and after every meeting Miriam rushed back to the hotel to change out of those chafing, feminine clothes, and into pants, or even overalls. The afternoons were rough going for both Miriam and Billy in Houston – and later in Dallas and Tulsa – for there was nothing for them to do, and both were used to hard work. At first they had maintained separate rooms, but after the first night they had decided to share a room. It wasn't that they needed to save money, but they hated waste.

The question of seduction had been set aside by Miriam's matter-of-factness when she said after the first night in Houston: 'You see what they're charging us for these rooms, Billy? And my room's got two beds. You come on in here tonight, and let that other room go. No sense in our taking fifteen dollars out of our pockets to put in theirs.' That night, on the telephone to her father, Miriam said, 'If Frances needs to speak to Billy, tell her that's he's staying here in my room. This hotel charges fifteen dollars a night, and we decided we were damned if we were paying for two rooms.'

'Miriam,' said her father, 'do you know that Billy snores?'

Billy was embarrassed at first that Miriam dressed and undressed right in front of him, until he realized that she never bothered to draw the shades either. She wasn't trying to seduce him or excite voyeurs in the neighboring buildings, she was simply unselfconscious and naturally immodest.

As he lay in bed that night, with Miriam asleep and snoring herself in the other bed, Billy wondered why he had chosen Frances rather than Miriam. It was an acknowledged fact in the family and in Perdido that Miriam was prettier. She was capable and smart, and Billy enjoyed her company. But she was like a sister to him, and Frances was definitely a wife. It was, he decided before he drifted off, another of those mysteries of the Caskey women.

In only one company out of the eight they visited were Miriam and Billy received with anything less than courtesy and interest. She let each of them know that she and Billy could be reached in about ten days or so in Perdido, but that they would be doing a little traveling until then.

'Let them stew,' said Miriam.

At the end of their mission, she and Billy drove from Tulsa to Little Rock on the first day. On the second day, starting very early, they made it to Jackson, Mississippi, before stopping at noon for something to eat. They turned in at a dilapidated barbecue restaurant with fragrant smoke coming out of a wide chimney. Both ordered pork ribs, French-fried onions and a beer.

After their meal they walked to the cash register and Billy paid their check. While he was waiting for his change, he was astonished to hear Miriam addressing the cook at the stove.

'What the hell are you doing back there?' she demanded in a sour voice.

Billy looked up. At the grill in back was a man about thirty, handsome in his way, but greasy and splattered with barbecue sauce, wearing a filthy apron and a dingy white shirt beneath that.

He had turned to Miriam with surprise and begun to reply automatically, 'Hey, ma'am, I'm—' when he broke off, and exclaimed, 'Miriam!'

'Get out from behind there,' commanded Miriam. 'This minute.'

'Miriam,' Billy said in a low voice, 'who—'

'Now just a second,' said the manager at the cash register, holding up a coarse fleshy hand.

The cook put down his spatula and came forward.

'Miriam?' he said again.

'Do you know who this is?' said Miriam angrily to Billy, paying no attention to the manager.

'Lord, no!' exclaimed Billy. 'I have no idea in the world, Miriam.'

'This is Malcolm. Malcolm Strickland, Queenie's son. Lucille's brother. Malcolm Strickland, what the hell do you think you're doing back there?'

'He's cooking for me!' said the manager indignantly, stretching out his hand to push Malcolm back toward the stove. 'And there are people waiting, Strickland.'

'Queenie thinks you are dead!' cried Miriam.

'She don't!'

'She does, 'cause you haven't written her in I-don't-know-how-many years. She thinks you probably got yourself killed in the Pacific somewhere. She looks at that picture of the flag-raising on Iwo Jima, and she says, "I wonder if one of those poor boys is Malcolm." Why the hell haven't you picked up the telephone and called her?'

Malcolm didn't answer, but he began to retreat toward the stove.

'Danjo joined the army,' said Miriam, raising her voice. 'He married a German girl called Fred and now they're living in a castle on the top of some damn mountain. Queenie is spending all her time nursing Sister. Sister fell down the stairs when Early Haskew came after her, and hasn't got out of the bed since that day.' Miriam's voice continued to rise in a crescendo. 'Lucille has a baby boy called Tommy Lee, and she and Tommy Lee are living with Grace out on a farm south of Babylon, and there's millions and millions of barrels of oil under a swamp out there.'

'Oil?' echoed Malcolm weakly, astounded by this unexpected flood of revelations in his family. He had imagined that in his absence, everything had remained the same.

'Malcolm Strickland,' said Miriam, her voice now low and threatening, 'get out from behind this counter, *right now*.'

All the customers in the restaurant – some thirty or more – had stopped all pretense of eating and were following the little drama at the counter.

'Strickland,' said the owner of the restaurant, 'you get back to that stove. Ma'am,' he said in exasperation to Miriam, 'why the hell don't you just take off?'

Miriam flipped up the board that allowed entrance behind the counter, marched past the astounded manager, grabbed Malcolm's greasy arm, and pulled him out past the register.

'Get the car started,' she said to Billy.

Billy, his change still on the counter, hurried out of the building. Miriam, with Malcolm in tow, headed after him.

'Leave the apron!' the restaurant owner shouted.

'Stand still,' Miriam ordered Malcolm, then she spun him around. Undoing and then removing the apron, she flung it over the back of a chair, and pulled Malcolm out the door.

'Get in the back seat,' she commanded once they'd got outside.

'Miriam, where on earth—' Malcolm began.

'I am taking you back to Perdido, where you belong.'

'Lord, Miriam, I cain't—'

He was already in the back seat.

'Are you married or something?' Miriam asked.

He shook his head.

'Have you bought a house?'

He shook his head again. 'I got my clothes though,' he ventured softly.

'Queenie'll buy you new ones,' said Miriam. 'Billy, let's go.'

The owner of the restaurant stood in the front entrance of the restaurant, shouting that Malcolm was fired and would never find work in Hinds County again.

Miriam turned around in the seat. 'James is dead – died a year ago – and left Queenie money.'

Malcolm stared out the window, as if riding in an automobile were a thing completely new to him.

'Your old friend Travis Gann is gone, too. You know what he did? He went and raped your sister, that's what he did, and she got pregnant. But that's a secret, so not a single word, you hear, Malcolm?'

Malcolm nodded his head.

And so the journey back to Perdido continued with Malcolm in the back seat. He could hardly overcome his bewilderment at being summarily kidnapped from his job and his life of three years past. While Billy drove steadily southeast through the corn and cotton fields of Mississippi, Miriam would occasionally turn around to throw some piece of family or town news at Malcolm or to berate him for his treatment of Queenie.

It was dark by the time they crossed the Alabama line, and Miriam had dozed off. 'Alabama,' Billy said, and Miriam shook herself awake. 'We'll be in Perdido in about an hour.'

Malcolm said, 'Miriam, you think Ma's gone want to see me?'

'Of course, she is,' snapped Miriam. 'But she's gone be mad to find out you're still alive.'

'I treated her bad,' said Malcolm.

'You sure did. Are you gone sponge off her for the rest of your life now?'

'Hey, I been working three years. I was in the army for six. I ain't been sponging off nobody.'

'You're no-good, Malcolm,' said Miriam. 'And you're never going to amount to anything. I don't know why I bothered to pull you out from behind that counter.'

'Neither do I,' sighed Malcolm from the darkness of the back seat.

The Caskeys were still at the table at Elinor's when Billy, Miriam, and Malcolm pulled up before the house that night.

'I don't want to go in,' said Malcolm.

'I wouldn't either if I smelled like you,' said Miriam, getting out of the car. 'Wait five minutes, Malcolm, and then come on inside. There's no sense in putting off and putting off.'

Billy and Miriam staggered wearily into the house. As they stepped into the dining room everyone rose from the table to welcome them. Knowing of their probable return that evening, Lucille and Grace and Tommy Lee had come in from Gavin Pond Farm. The outcome of the trip to Texas would affect them most.

'This family has been falling apart!' exclaimed Queenie.

Frances embraced her husband.

'Did y'all bring us a million dollars in cash?' asked Grace facetiously.

'No,' returned Miriam. 'What we brought back was a plugged nickel.'

'Oh,' said Queenie, 'that's too bad. We got the impression everything was going along pretty well.'

'There's no problem about the oil,' said Miriam airily, 'I imagine my phone'll start ringing tomorrow.'

'The phone started ringing two days ago,' said Oscar, 'but I told them that you were still out of town and there wasn't anybody else they could talk to.'

Billy, still holding his wife close, looked over Frances's shoulder, and said, 'Miriam and I have got a surprise out in the car.'

'Oh,' cried Queenie excitedly. 'Y'all brought us presents. I bet it's moccasins, and Indian stuff. Y'all were in Oklahoma, weren't you? You know I've got a brother in Oklahoma, I haven't heard from Pony in—'

Queenie broke off at the sound of the front screen door banging shut.

'Who is that?' asked Elinor.

'That,' Miriam replied, 'is the surprise.'

In the doorway stood Malcolm, dingy, rumpled, wan, smelling of rancid grease and barbecue sauce.

Queenie screamed and collapsed into her chair.

'Oh, Lord!' cried Lucille, and jumped behind her mother's chair as if she needed protection.

'We thought you were dead,' said Grace in a low voice.

'Well, he's not,' said Miriam. 'Found him outside of Jackson, looking just about like he does now except he had an apron on then. Malcolm, now that everybody's seen you, maybe you could do us all a favor and go over to Queenie's and take a bath.'

'What'll I wear when I get out of the tub?' said the bewildered Malcolm, glancing down at his clothes. He looked around the room at his family, and explained, 'She wouldn't stop. I guess she thought I'd run away. I wouldn't have. I sort of missed Perdido. Miriam said James was dead. That's too bad.' Then he turned and shuffled out into the darkness of the hallway.

Queenie screamed again and ran after him. 'Malcolm! Malcolm!'

'He's all grown up!' marveled Grace to Lucille. 'I cain't hardly believe it.'

'If y'all had told me,' said unperturbed Zaddie, coming into the dining room from the kitchen, 'I would have killed the fatted calf.'

NEW YEAR'S

Though she was bone weary, Miriam was up late the night of her return from Texas. Sister wouldn't let her go to bed. Sister was angry that Miriam had stayed away so long. Sister was mad that Miriam had telephoned so infrequently. Sister first wanted to hear Miriam tell one story, about her success with the oil companies for instance, but almost as quickly as Miriam had begun it, Sister interrupted with a demand for another tale altogether. 'Tell me what you thought when you saw Malcolm standing at that stove in the barbecue restaurant, darling.' Sister's mind wouldn't stay fixed. One minute she would be demanding that Miriam walk across the room and hug her, and the next Sister would almost weep for her own unhappiness at being abandoned for such a protracted time.

'You know what happened to me when you were gone?' Sister said accusingly.

'What?' said Miriam wearily, sitting in a wicker chair next to the door, as if to make a very quick exit if Sister would ever let her go.

'You know who walked in this house right through the front screen door and nobody lifted a finger to stop him from doing it?'

'Who?'

'Early. Early walked right in the door in the middle of the night. Walked right in this room one night and said, "Sister, come back to Mobile with me." Tried to pull me out of the bed. I said, "Early, my legs will crumble right under me and you will have a mess on your hands." I told him, "Early, I'm a cripple." He said, "You're not," and said, "When you get out of that bed, I'm coming to get you."'

Miriam's head lolled. She scarcely followed Sister's report.

'So you know what that means?' cried Sister angrily.

'What?' murmured Miriam.

'It means *I will never leave this bed again. That's* what it means.'

This did get Miriam's attention, and she looked up. 'You don't mean that.'

'I do.'

'You are in that bed waiting for your leg to mend. You should have been up a month ago at the least.'

'I'm never gone leave this bed,' Sister repeated

adamantly. 'Not if Early Haskew is in his car parked out front looking in my windows with field glasses waiting to see me hobble down the hall so he can run in and get me.'

'Early's not going to come and get you,' said Miriam. 'He cain't take you away if you don't want to go.'

'We're married!'

'Doesn't make any difference,' said Miriam, shaking her head.

'Fix my pillows,' said Sister.

'I will not,' said Miriam, her strength returning with her anger. 'If you think for one minute that you are going to lie in that bed and be waited on by all of us for the rest of your life, giving up our comfort and our free time in order to plump your pillows and empty your bed pans and bring you magazines, you are sadly mistaken, Sister.'

'My leg hurts so bad, Miriam! Why do you want to talk to me like that? Why do you want to say harsh words to an old crippled woman like me? An old crippled woman who cain't even get out of the bed to go to the bathroom when she has to go?'

'You're no more crippled than I am,' said Miriam, now totally revived. 'If I were smart, what I'd do is drive you way out in the country, open the car door and push you out and make you *walk* back to Perdido.'

'You'd do it too, wouldn't you!' cried Sister. 'I bet you would, for meanness' sake.'

'I'm not the mean one anymore,' remarked Miriam. 'I'm not the one who makes Queenie stay over here with me seven hours a day when she could be doing whatever she wanted to be doing in her own house. I'm not the one who makes it impossible for Ivey to get any work done because she has to run upstairs every three minutes to do something for the cripple in the bed. I'm not the one who keeps somebody up far into the night, somebody who's just come back from a long hard trip.'

'That's me, I suppose. I suppose you're talking about me.'

'I am,' declared Miriam, rising.

Sister picked up a magazine of crossword puzzles from her bedside table and flung it at Miriam. It sailed through the air and struck Miriam on the inside of her elbow.

'Good-night to you, too,' said Miriam and stalked out of the room.

Sister screamed out: 'Miriam, wait! Wait!'

Miriam marched down the hall and turned back only when she had reached the door of her room.

Peering down to the end of the hall and in through the open doorway of Sister's room, she saw Sister struggle to get out of the bed. She watched as Sister pushed aside the mountain of pillows on which she had rested for so long and with a loud groan turn herself sideways on the bed and force her legs off the side.

'Miriam!' Sister called.

'I'm here.'

Sister slid carefully off the side of the bed until her feet touched the floor. Gradually she increased her weight on them until she let go the bed, which she had been using as support.

'See!' cried Miriam. 'You're not a cripple.'

Sister took a step toward the hallway. Then another. Suddenly her left leg jackknifed and she dropped to the floor in a heap. Her pale brow hit the polished wooden floor with a resounding thud.

Miriam ran back down the hall and into the room. She gathered Sister up – it was no difficulty, as Sister was woefully thin – and lifted her back onto the bed. Then, one limb at a time, Miriam made Sister comfortable on the high mattress, arranging the covers over her and the pillows behind her. She wet a cloth in the bathroom and bathed the bump on Sister's forehead.

'Fix my pillows,' Sister groaned. Miriam did so.

'Are you all right now?'

'No,' said Sister. 'You have just turned me into a living temple of pain.'

'Do you want me to call Leo Benquith?'

'What good could he do? Call Queenie.'

'Not at this time of night with Malcolm just back!'

'I know they're up over there, they're bound to be, with you bringing Malcolm back and all.'

'I'm not going to ask Queenie to come over here at one o'clock in the morning,' said Miriam.

'She'll come,' said Sister confidently. 'She always does.'

Miriam said nothing. She merely turned and walked out of the room.

Sister picked up the telephone, and while waiting for the operator to come on, she called out to the retreating Miriam, 'See, I told you I was a cripple.'

Despite the lateness of the hour, as Sister had predicted, everyone in Queenie's household was still up when Sister called. Queenie had taken Malcolm home, pushed him into the bedroom, pressed him into the bathroom, received his reeking clothes through the cracked door, shoved others in, and actually sat on the edge of the bed biting her fingernails while Malcolm bathed away the smell of grease and barbecue sauce and replaced it with the fragrance of the best of James's scented soaps.

Afterward, with Malcolm squeezed tightly into a pair of Oscar's trousers and one of his shirts, the reunited family sat in the living room staring at one another. Grace had taken Tommy Lee back to Gavin Pond Farm, but had left Lucille at her mother's. 'I want to hear what Malcolm has got to say for himself,' said Lucille. 'Four years and not one word!'

Malcolm, it turned out, had little to say. He had been in the army, which they all knew. He had trained in North Dakota, fought in Italy, and been honorably discharged in Massachusetts. He had learned two skills: bricklaying and cooking for crowds. After leaving the army, he had laid brick sidewalks in Boston, but union difficulties had relieved him of that job. He had come south and found work with a contracting firm in Little Rock. Fired from a job the company was working on in Jackson, he had picked up work at a downtown diner. The barbecue restaurant had been his fourth position as cook.

'Doesn't sound like you were building up much of a homelife,' remarked Lucille, to whom homelife had become important.

'I was not,' said Malcolm contritely.

'*This* is your home,' said Queenie.

Malcolm did not answer, but it appeared to his mother and sister that he was not denying the proposition. His silence implied he felt unworthy of his mother's kindness.

'You think Oscar or somebody could find me some work around here?' he asked.

'Doing what?' Queenie asked.

'Cooking, maybe. Or laying bricks.'

'Which do you like better?' asked Lucille.

Malcolm shrugged. 'Don't much matter to me.'

'Lord,' said Queenie, 'I'm sure they can find you *something*, Malcolm. I don't know, maybe they're gone want to brick in the levee or something. I just want to know, Malcolm—'

'What, Ma?'

'If we *did* find you something, would you stay around? And be good? And *work* at it, whatever it was?'

'Oh, Ma,' said Malcolm softly. 'You don't know me no more. See, what you remember about me is that trial and getting in trouble with Travis Gann and all that and almost going to jail. See, that's what you think when you call me up in your mind. But that's not me anymore. I wasn't even twenty years old then. Now I'm almost thirty. I was in the army six years and four months. And I've been here and I've been there, holding down jobs, meeting people. Bricklaying's all right when it's nice out, but not in the sun. Cooking's all right if you don't mind smelling of grease and always being sweaty and dirty. There was times I got fired, and I got fired 'cause I got mad or somebody got mad at me and we got in a fight or something, but most of the time it wasn't my fault. I'd tell you if it was, but it wasn't. Ma, you probably think I was away ten years and I got to be just like Pa was. But I'm not like him. I never went to jail, I wasn't arrested but once and that was up in Boston in a bar, and that wasn't even my fight. That was somebody else's fight and they just hauled us all off. That's all that was. So I see y'all looking at me like "Who's he gone beat up next?" and "Who'd he kill last week?" but that's not it.'

Queenie, who had been sitting at the other end of the sofa from Malcolm, jumped suddenly closer and embraced him.

'I know it's not! I always knew it wasn't!'

Malcolm laughed. 'No, you didn't. Did she, Lucille? You thought I was wasting away in a state pen somewhere, that's what you thought, wasn't it, Ma?'

Queenie shook her head. 'I thought you died on Iwo Jima.'

Sister called then, demanding Queenie's presence. Queenie pressed her weary son into bed, and then went next door and heard Sister's complaints until dawn.

The next day, Queenie took Malcolm to Pensacola and bought him new clothes. He was alarmed by the amount of money she spent on him and protested against such prodigality.

'Malcolm,' Queenie protested, 'I've got the money. What better thing can I do with it than spend it on my children? Malcolm, you want me to buy you this whole store? 'Cause I could!'

At subsequent meals at Elinor's, Malcolm's future

was discussed at length. Bricklaying and cooking for large groups were not skills demanded by Perdido, and anyway Queenie thought it was time Malcolm had a respectable job. Malcolm's skills, though, were meager, employment was scarce, and nobody – it seemed for a time – had any use for him. The weeks went by, and time hung heavy on Malcolm's hands.

When he was very busy, Billy Bronze would call up Malcolm and ask him to run down to Pensacola or Mobile and deliver papers or pick up papers or transact some small piece of business. Malcolm consented, and Queenie usually went along for the ride. Billy told Miriam about Malcolm's usefulness, and she employed him in a similar manner to carry cash out to a farmer in Washington County who distrusted checks or to deliver a bushel of fresh corn from Gavin Pond Farm to the wife of the Representative to Congress.

Malcolm became known in the family for his willingness to perform these trivial but time-consuming and inconvenient errands. Soon he was doing jobs for Elinor and Sister as well. If a gutter came down in a storm, Malcolm arranged for someone to come and fix it. If a dress bought in Mobile was the wrong size, Malcolm returned it. If train tickets were needed, Malcolm drove up to Atmore and got the right ones. He kept the Caskey cars serviced and filled with gas. He made sure wood and coal were ordered, and he swatted the bats that sometimes flew down Elinor's chimneys. He was unable to repair a carpet sweeper himself, but he could be certain that the job was done within the day. If anything went wrong in any of the Caskey houses, the Caskeys sat back and said, 'Somebody call up Malcolm and tell him to take care of it.' By the end of the summer Malcolm was as busy as Miriam and Billy in their offices. He had become a sort of major domo to the Caskeys, and they began to wonder how they had ever done without him. Billy offered him a salary.

'But what is my job?' he asked. 'I'm happy to do all these things, 'cause I'm really not doing anything else.'

'Keeping things going smoothly is worth money, Malcolm,' said Billy. 'And we can afford to pay you. Take the money.'

The Caskeys scarcely remembered the old Malcolm with this new Malcolm before them. It was universally agreed that he must have had a difficult time away from Perdido. He was quiet, but he wasn't meek; he was controlled. His temper remained, but when he felt it rising over some perceived slight or contretemps, he would walk away, fling large rocks at the nearest object unlikely to be injured by such an attack, slug down a bottle of warm beer from a case that he always kept in the back of the car, and soon he was placid again. At times his moodiness was of longer duration. He then kept to his room. Queenie would put food on a tray and leave it outside his door. No one attempted to coax him out, and afterward no one asked what the trouble was.

Miriam treated Malcolm as she treated everyone: offhandedly, impatiently, and with a sometimes grueling forthrightness. Queenie cringed at some of the things Miriam said to her son, but Malcolm defended Miriam: 'What she says is right, Mama, and you know it.'

'She doesn't have to say it out loud, though, Malcolm, and certainly not where other people can hear it.'

Miriam was busy. The oil companies had, with one exception, telephoned, asking for more information. The executives could scarcely believe that Miriam on the telephone from her office in Perdido was the same 'hapless' lady in the feminine dresses who had sighed and protested in their offices in Texas and Oklahoma. To them all, Miriam said, 'You're not the only ones interested. Send a man out here to see me first, and I'll show him what's what. Then you can send somebody else to talk money.'

She wouldn't listen to first offers of contracts for exploratory drilling. The men on the phone always attempted to persuade her: 'Let us handle it all for you, Miss Caskey.'

'No, thank you,' Miriam would reply crisply. 'If you're really interested, send me a geologist, an engineer, an accountant, and a lawyer. And then we'll talk some business.'

And so over the next few weeks, men of those professions began arriving in Perdido, at staggered intervals, and were put up at the Osceola Hotel. Miriam and Malcolm would drive them out to Gavin Pond Farm and introduce them to Grace and Lucille. In two small boats with motors, Malcolm and Grace guided the oil company men through the swamp. Miriam would sit in the prow of one boat and Lucille in the prow of the other, holding aloft paddles to beat off alligators and water moccasins. Miriam was no longer frightened of the swamp, because she perceived it to be in the interests of business.

Miriam knew these trips were unnecessary, because her own geologists' and engineers' reports were sufficient. She wanted, however, to find out something about the differences in the oil companies, and did not see a better way of doing this than by meeting their chosen representatives.

A month after her return from Texas, Miriam and the other Caskeys signed a preliminary contract allowing Texas National Oil to drill two exploratory wells in the swamp. Theirs was not the highest bid but, certain that there was oil beneath the swamp, Miriam had been more interested in contracting for favorable percentages after the oil had been found and extracted. Texas National raised the Caskey royalty schedule two points in exchange for Miriam's agreement to bear the cost of one of the two exploratory wells. It was anticipated that six months' time would be required to work out details and to transport the proper machinery to Florida, where no one had ever drilled before.

'Those things cost a lot of money,' said Oscar at supper the evening following the final signing of the papers. 'Are you sure that was a smart thing to do?'

Miriam shrugged. 'We'll make it up in the first year from the percentage they're offering.'

'*If* there's oil,' Oscar pointed out.

'Elinor says there is,' said Miriam, glancing at her mother across the table. 'And that's what I'm going on. If we all end up at the poor farm, y'all can blame Elinor and not me.'

Because of the mill, the town bustled and thrived, while the Perdido and Blackwater rivers flowed so peacefully and out of sight beyond the red levees. Frances Caskey swam in the Perdido every day – that was known in town, and a fact sometimes used as an argument by ten- and eleven-year-old boys whose parents had placed the river off-limits.

'Frances Caskey,' their parents pointed out, 'was

teaching swimming out at Lake Pinchona before you were born, and if her family wants to let her risk her life every afternoon, they can. But *you*, young man, are not going to be sucked down to the bottom of the junction. That is that.'

These parents didn't know, however, of the time-honored custom among boys in Perdido of skinny-dipping in the river on New Year's Day. The ritual was not exactly pleasant, for the water was cold at the beginning of January. Among the boys, however, this rite was both a statement of imagined independence and a kind of dare brought about by the experience and example of older brothers. A spot south of town, where the Perdido is wide and shallow, was usually chosen; not even ten-year-olds wanted to risk the danger of being sucked into the whirlpool at the junction. On New Year's Day of 1948, seven young Perdido boys sneaked out of their houses at nine o'clock in the morning and variously made their way to the clandestine place. The day was overcast and chilly as they shucked their jackets, shirts, suspenders, trousers, and underwear. One by one they dived into the water, employing the broken-off trunk of a fallen tree for a springboard. The water was colder than any of them imagined, and the boys' teeth chattered in the water even as they shouted for their reluctant companions to jump in. Finally, even the most timid boy had slipped down the muddy bank and flailed screaming into the cold muddy water. The seven boys swam around, bared their chattering teeth, dunked and splashed about, and eventually agreed that it was time to get out.

Six boys scrambled up the muddy bank.

The seventh – the younger Gully boy, whose father owned Perdido's car dealership – was missing. His friends ran up and down the bank, calling his name frantically. They plied the water with long sticks; they screamed into the air imprecations against him for scaring them so; they stared helplessly at the swiftly flowing muddy water and swore a blood oath that none of them would reveal that they had been a party to the disappearance of their companion. They knew their parents would never allow them out of the house again. They crept home by various routes, ready with elaborate excuses – trembling victims of guilt.

By the end of that day, Mrs Gully realized that her boy was missing. A great hue and cry went up. The other six boys, his friends, were questioned. Their teeth chattered as they spoke the lie, but each maintained he knew nothing at all. The missing boy's clothing was found on the banks of the Perdido, and the Gullys were astonished that their son seemed to have gone swimming, alone, on New Year's Day. The Gullys, who had lived in Perdido all their lives, knew how many children those red, muddy waters had swallowed already. They did not expect to see their son again. An old man with a grappling hook was sent out on the river for a few days, but that was only for form's sake and the comfort of the grandparents in Mississippi. The Perdido, everyone knew, never gave up its dead.

New Year's Day of 1948 was a Thursday. That evening at supper Frances Bronze had appeared troubled, and after the meal, when most everyone was in the front parlor, Elinor motioned to her daughter to follow her upstairs.

'What is wrong, darling?' said Elinor, as she ushered her daughter into her bedroom and closed the door. Frances sat on the edge of her parents' bed and glanced out the window at the mass of water oaks.

'Little boy died today, Mama. Gully boy.'

'I heard they were looking for him,' said Elinor guardedly. 'I didn't hear they had found him.'

'They haven't found him,' said Frances slowly. 'They won't.'

Elinor went to the window. 'Nerita?' she asked.

'Yes,' said Frances.

When Elinor turned around, Frances was weeping softly.

'Darling,' said Elinor, 'these things happen.'

'I told her not to do something like that! I told her never to go *near* people in the water. Why cain't she just eat fish! She *loves* catfish.'

'Well,' said Elinor softly, 'you cain't make a whole diet out of catfish.'

'Mama!'

Elinor sat beside Frances and put her arm around her. 'Listen, honey, you've got to remember. Nerita's not like you and me. You and I can get along pretty well on Dollie's beef and pork and veal – and Malcolm's venison when he goes out in the woods and shoots a deer. But where is Nerita going to get pork and beef and veal and venison? She's a big girl now, but she's still growing. She probably thought she needed it—'

'Mama! What if they started hunting for her!'

Elinor smiled. 'They couldn't find her, darling. Nerita would just sit at the bottom of the junction until they went away. I'd like to see somebody try to pull anything up out of *there*.'

'Aren't you upset about the Gully boy, Mama? You know that boy's parents, and they're real sweet. Queenie is *always* buying a new car from that man, and he's always so polite to us.'

'Of course, I'm sorry for them,' said Elinor. 'But there's nothing we can do. And what was that boy doing in the river on New Year's Day anyway? It's cold out there!'

'Nerita said there were a bunch of them down there, below town. She said' – here Frances grimaced – 'that she could have gotten them all if she had wanted to.'

Elinor smiled, and there was something of pride in it. She said, 'There's no stopping that girl, is there?'

'No, ma'am.'

Mother and daughter were silent for a few moments.

'There's something else bothering you, isn't there?'

Frances nodded.

'What is it?'

'I don't think I want to tell.'

'But you'll tell anyway, won't you? Otherwise, you wouldn't have come up here with me. You wouldn't have told me anything, if you weren't going to tell me everything. What is it?'

'Nerita didn't eat all of the Gully boy.'

'No?' said Elinor.

'No, *she saved me part.*'

BILLY'S ARMOR

Since his return from Texas, Billy Bronze had noticed a change in his wife. 'Distant' didn't seem quite the word for it, 'preoccupied' was more like it – and preoccupied with something besides their infant daughter Lilah. He wondered at first whether he hadn't angered Frances by going away for two weeks with her sister. He asked her about this.

'Frances,' he said carefully one morning while he was dressing for work and she was changing the baby's diaper, 'you know what I wish?'

'What?'

'I wish I hadn't gone off with Miriam to Texas.'

'Why not?' asked Frances. 'Miriam said she needed you.'

'She didn't, though. She did everything just fine all by herself.'

'Then she needed you for company. Deep down inside Miriam's not as independent as everybody thinks she is. As *she* thinks she is. So you were keeping her company, and letting her know that she was doing things right.'

'Then it doesn't bother you that I went?'

Frances looked up in surprise. 'Were you thinking that it bothered me? Why should it bother me?'

'I don't know,' returned Billy lamely. ''Cause you might have thought . . .'

'Thought what?' asked Frances in perplexity. Then suddenly she realized what he meant. 'That something was going on?'

Billy nodded.

Frances laughed. 'You and Miriam? What a thing to say, Billy!'

'Why is it such a thing to say?'

'Because if you had wanted Miriam instead of me, then you'd be married to her. You had your choice when you first came to Perdido. And if Miriam had wanted you, why you'd be over next door and *Miriam* would be the one changing diapers. *That's* why it's such a funny thing to say. Billy, you don't really think I was imagining that something was going on between you two, do you? Wait'll I tell Mama, won't she laugh out loud!'

Billy was perplexed by his wife's attitude. He hadn't thought the thing quite so improbable as Frances was making it out to be.

'We slept in the same hotel room,' he pointed out.

'Everybody knows what Miriam is like when it comes to spending money. She wasn't gone *let* you have a separate room – I knew that when you two took off. Lord, Billy, she's my *sister*.' Frances pulled open her housecoat, and pressed Lilah against her left breast. Sitting down in the platform rocker in the corner of her room next to the porch window she began to rock. Lilah fed with her eyes closed contentedly.

'Well,' said Billy, 'if that's not what's been bothering you, what *has* it been?'

'What are you talking about now?'

'You've been thinking about something else.'

'When?'

'All the time. Everytime somebody says something to you, it's got to be repeated, 'cause you're never listening. You don't think about Lilah until she starts to cry, or unless Zaddie comes up here and tells you it's time to feed her. You're always standing at the window and looking out at the levee, like there was something real important on your mind. Darling, I just want to know if there's something I can help with.'

Frances was silent a moment, then turned serious. She responded in a quiet voice, that had something in its tone that indicated to her husband that this was not a lie, but an evasion. 'It's nothing, Billy. No, I tell you what it is, it's being a mother. It's new to me. It's strange. I wasn't prepared. I'm always thinking about my little girl.'

Billy laughed uneasily. 'Then why does she always need changing every time I pick her up?'

'See?' said Frances hastily. 'I'm not used to it yet. I'm not sure exactly how things are supposed to be done. That's all. Pretty soon I'll figure out exactly what I'm supposed to do.'

This exchange did not entirely satisfy Billy Bronze. And his unease increased when he returned to the house one afternoon and discovered Elinor on the porch with Lilah gently sleeping in her lap.

'Where's Frances?' he asked, looking about the porch as if his wife might have been hiding behind the pyramid of ferns in the corner or crouching behind the glider.

'Oh,' Elinor replied vaguely, 'she went off somewhere . . .'

'How long has she been gone?'

'Awhile.'

'She shouldn't run off and make you take care of Lilah.'

'Lord, Billy, I don't mind! I love this baby! I wish I had this baby all for my own!'

At that moment, he heard his wife's footsteps on the hall stairs. He went to the porch door to meet her as she came up. He was astounded to find her wet and bedraggled, barefooted, her teeth chattering in the crisp February air.

'What the hell have you been doing?' he exclaimed.

'Swimming,' replied Frances.

'In weather like this? It's freezing out there.'

'In the water I'm fine,' breathed Frances, trying to edge past her husband to get to their room. 'It's only when I get out that I'm cold.'

Billy followed her into the bathroom. Frances dropped her robe and ran hot water into the tub.

'I'm covered with mud,' she said, and that was the truth.

'How long were you out there, Frances? I called here right after dinner and Zaddie said you weren't here. It's four o'clock now – you were swimming in the Perdido for *three hours?*'

Frances shrugged, and stepped gingerly into the hot water. 'You know how it is, Billy, you lose track of the time. And Mama *loves* taking care of Lilah. You want to wash my hair?'

In the following months matters only grew worse, as far as Billy could see. He was very busy with the oil companies; there was another visit to Texas with Miriam and then he went a third time on his own. Each trip lasted several days. Frances grew more and more distant from him and their daughter, even though she denied that anything had changed. Elinor denied it, too. Billy realized that Lilah had been placed in almost complete care of his mother-in-law and Zaddie. Frances weaned Lilah at eight months, and shortly thereafter Lilah's basinet was moved downstairs with Zaddie. 'Her crying keeps me awake,' Frances explained. 'There have been nights when I couldn't get to sleep at all.'

Frances seemed to be developing an actual abhorrence to her daughter. She never talked about her, never picked her up, never played with her. When Billy spoke of Lilah, Frances changed the subject. When Billy picked Lilah up, Frances turned her head. When Billy played with Lilah, Frances left the room on a lame excuse. He mentioned these things to Elinor, but she as usual denied there was a problem. If Billy saw anything wrong, said Elinor, it must be that he was working too hard, or was experiencing the inevitable letdown that follows childbirth, or perhaps it was the effects of the bad winter weather. In other words, any cause that had nothing to do with Frances.

If ever Billy telephoned home in the afternoon, wanting to speak to Frances, she was never there. This was true whether he called right after he had returned to his office after lunch, or in the middle of the afternoon, or half an hour before he was to come home. Elinor always told him that she was out shopping, or at the seamstress's, or delivering a pound cake to somebody who was sick. Whenever Billy sought to verify any of these stories, Frances said, 'Oh, no, Mama was wrong. I just drove out to

Dollie Faye's to pick up some bacon. I walked in the door right after Mama hung up the phone.'

Sometimes at night, after they had turned out the light, Billy would turn on his pillow and beg Frances to tell him what was the matter with her, why she was acting in this way.

'Nothing is the matter, Billy, nothing at all.'

He had thought at first that hers might be a physical ailment and urged her to see either Leo Benquith or the new doctor in town. Frances wouldn't go. 'Nothing is wrong with me, Billy. I feel fine.'

And, in fact, Frances seemed to grow healthier by the day. Billy was startled almost beyond words to discover that she seemed to be growing – Frances was now almost as tall as he! He made her stand against the doorframe of their room and he marked her height with a pencil. Then he stood against the frame and she marked his. Her mark was only an inch or two short of his.

'I *know*,' he exclaimed, 'that when we got married, you were a good five inches shorter than me.'

'I'm wearing my hair different,' Frances explained. 'And I do stretching exercises.'

She seemed to be getting stronger, too. One morning after breakfast Billy had started out the front door on his way to work, but then spun around and went back inside, having forgotten some letters on his dresser. He went upstairs, walked down the hall, and was about to enter the bedroom when he was stopped dead in his tracks by what he saw. Frances was crouched at the corner of the bed, and with a single hand she was lifting the bed at the corner, reaching for something that had apparently rolled under it. He watched astonished as she retrieved a pearl earring and gently set the bed back in place.

'Frances!' he cried. 'You are gone break your back doing something like that!'

Standing up, Frances merely remarked, 'Oh, that old bed just looks heavy. It's not really.'

Billy went over, placed his hand on the bedpost and attempted to lift it. For his pains he got a cramp in his upper arm.

Billy made a fourth trip to Houston, again with Miriam, in April 1948. This time Malcolm drove, while Billy and Miriam sat in the back of the new Cadillac that Billy had bought for the family, looked over papers and correspondence, and endlessly talked strategy. On each of the six days they were in Texas Billy telephoned his wife. Three times she was not at home, once she was sleeping and Zaddie refused to wake her, and twice he was able to speak to her briefly. On this trip Billy and Malcolm shared a room, and Miriam had one to herself.

'Miriam,' he said to his sister-in-law over before-dinner drinks on the night before they were to return to Perdido. 'I don't know what I'm going to do.'

'About what?' Miriam asked. Miriam had decided that on this last evening, with everything accomplished that needed to be accomplished, she and Malcolm and Billy would celebrate by going out to Houston's best restaurant. Miriam wore a new dress, and she had minutely supervised Malcolm into a new suit. She kept an eagle eye on his manners at the table, and had said, 'Don't bother looking at the menu, Malcolm, I'm going to order for you.'

'About Frances,' Billy went on, after the waiter had taken their orders. 'Frances – haven't you noticed – has changed since Lilah was born.'

'How?' asked Malcolm.

'How?' asked Miriam.

'Just . . . changed.' Billy shrugged. 'Does funny things. Doesn't pay any attention to Lilah. Zaddie and Elinor are raising that baby. I think the only time Frances even holds that child is when I'm home and I actually pick Lilah up and put her in Frances's arms.'

'Maybe Frances doesn't like babies,' suggested Miriam. 'I don't think I would.'

'I don't think she likes *Lilah*,' said Billy. 'It's almost like she thinks she got hold of the wrong one, and this is a substitute and she doesn't want anything to do with it.'

'Maybe she's mad 'cause you're always going off to Texas,' said Miriam.

'She says she isn't.'

'Malcolm,' said Miriam, 'get the waiter's attention. And try to do it without standing up and waving your arms over your head.'

Malcolm nodded to the waiter. He came to the table and Miriam ordered another round of drinks.

The second drink loosened Billy's tongue more. 'You know what else she does?'

Miriam shook her head. 'What?'

'She thinks I don't know she does it.'

'What does she do?' asked Malcolm.

'She goes swimming every day in the Perdido. She swims in the Perdido for hours and hours.'

'She gets that from Elinor,' Miriam pointed out. 'You ought to blame Elinor for that.'

'She did it even in the winter,' Billy said. 'Even that one day it was so cold the pipes froze, Frances went swimming in the Perdido. I call up in the afternoon, and she's never there. Elinor always gives me some excuse or Zaddie makes something up about where she is, but I *know* where she is. She's swimming in that damn river. I could go up to the top of that levee and look down and there'd be Frances, swimming round and round in water that would freeze a man's . . .'

'. . . balls off,' said Malcolm, completing the thought.

'You've seen her swimming?' asked Miriam, while glancing balefully at Malcolm.

'No, but I know she does it.'

'I don't see what difference it makes,' Miriam said.

'It makes a difference!' cried Billy. 'And I don't know why either. 'Cause she won't tell me that's what she does. 'Cause she won't have anything to do with Lilah. 'Cause I'm afraid,' he said in a low voice, 'that one of these days she's going to up and get a divorce with a Mobile lawyer.'

'Divorce you!' exclaimed Miriam.

'Well, she obviously doesn't love me anymore. If she loved me, she'd love our little girl. She wouldn't always be lying to me. She'd tell me what the real trouble is. I thought she loved me.'

'I thought she did too,' said Miriam. 'But what if she doesn't?'

'Then she'll want to get rid of me,' said Billy.

'Not necessarily,' Miriam pointed out. 'Maybe she'd let you stay on.'

Billy shook his head. 'Miriam, don't you understand? I love this family. I don't want to leave Perdido. See, *that's* what I'm afraid of, that Frances will want to get rid of me, and will make me get out of town.'

Miriam laughed. 'Billy, is that what you're worried about? You really think we'd let you go? Even if you and Frances did get a divorce, Elinor doesn't want to get rid of you. She'd just have you move into the front room. And if Frances doesn't want you in the house, then you can come live with Sister and me, that's all.

We're not gone let you leave town. That's the silliest thing I ever heard a grown man say. Malcolm, don't crunch your ice.'

Billy looked at Miriam perplexed.

'I cain't run this thing single-handed,' said Miriam. The liquor was loosening her tongue, too. She shook her head. 'Oscar's no good. He's backing out. He doesn't do anything anymore. He leaves everything to me. He's got one man out in the yard and another man out in the forests, and those two make all the decisions. Oscar just wanders around talking to people. He goes down to the barbershop and listens to all the gossip. They've got a back room down there that nobody's supposed to know about, and those old men sit back there and play dominoes all afternoon, a penny a point. And Oscar thinks I don't know about it. So what would I do without you, Billy? How could I handle all this on my own?'

'I'd help you, Miriam,' put in Malcolm. 'I'd be glad to help.'

'You're no help,' returned Miriam. 'I have to watch you every minute. I need Billy, working away downtown in his little office. I've got to have somebody to talk all this business over with. This is business I cain't think through all by myself. So, Billy, if Frances divorces you, I'll marry you myself. We aren't gone be letting you go, so you might as well get *that* out of your mind right now.'

The first course was brought, and there was no more talk of Frances. In a low voice Miriam instructed Malcolm in the intricacies of eating Clams Casino and what to do with the shells.

Billy's great fear had been that he would be banished from the Caskeys if Frances declared their marriage finished. He had seen what Sister had done to Early. Billy had always considered himself married to the clan, as if the Caskeys were one great bride and Frances were only the ring-bearing representative. Miriam had reassured him that if worse came to worst and Frances removed that ring, Miriam would pick it up and place it on her own finger.

Armed with this thought, he returned to Perdido. Malcolm parked in front of Miriam's house and began unloading the bags. Billy went immediately to his own home and called out his wife's name.

Zaddie pushed open the screen door for him and held a finger to her lips.

'Is the baby asleep?' he asked.

'No,' said Zaddie, 'Miss Frances sick in the bed.'

This did not tally with how he had imagined his homecoming; Billy hurried up the stairs. The door of his and Frances's bedroom was closed but he went in without knocking. The shades were drawn and the curtains closed; the room was nearly dark.

'Close the door!' cried Elinor. She was sitting in the

mahogany rocker at the side of the bed. Billy pushed the door shut behind him.

In the darkness, he could scarcely make out his wife in the bed. Despite the warmth of the evening, she lay under thick covers. She shifted and slid on the sheets.

'Hey, Billy,' Frances murmured.

'What's wrong with you?' he asked. 'Zaddie said you were sick.'

'Oh, I'm all right,' she replied in a weak voice. 'I'm just not feeling well right now.'

'Elinor, what's wrong with her?'

'My baby's just not up to par,' replied Elinor. 'She'll be all right. She missed you. Did you and Miriam get everything done all right?'

'Yes, ma'am,' replied Billy absently. 'What does the doctor say?'

'Nothing,' replied Frances. 'I don't need any doctor, I just need a little rest. I got tired out while you were gone, Billy. I need to stay in bed for a while, that's all. Listen, I hope you don't mind, but we moved some of your things into the front room. It's hard for me to sleep right now, and I cain't have anybody else in the bed with me. I'll be all right in a couple of days. Then we'll move everything right back in. I missed you a lot.'

There was, in Frances's voice, something soft and loving. It had been so long since Billy had heard her speak so, that he nearly wept from the surprise and tenderness of it.

'Sure, sure, and I missed you.'

'Billy,' said Elinor, 'why don't you go unpack? Frances is going to try to go to sleep now.'

'Bye, Billy,' said Frances weakly. 'I sure am glad you're back.'

'I'm just gone be in the next room, honey,' Billy assured her. 'You call and I'll hear you.'

Elinor rose from her chair and saw Billy out into the hallway.

'Is she really all right?' he whispered.

Elinor smiled and nodded. 'She'll be fine in a day or two.'

Elinor walked back into the bedroom.

'Is he gone?' Frances asked in a whisper.

'Well, he's not *gone*,' replied Elinor. 'He's just in the next room. And I am still mad at you, darling.'

'Mama, I told you, I couldn't help it!'

'You could have. You know better than to stay in that water as long as you did. You worried me to death. Now see what happened?'

'I didn't know it would happen.'

'I told you, darling, over and over again, you can't stay in the Perdido for more than a few hours.'

'I am stifling, Mama,' said Frances, pushing back the covers. Her powerful gray legs slipped wetly around on the sheets, and her webbed gray feet stretched and waggled now that they were no longer confined beneath the heavy blankets. Frances turned a little, and her powerful gray tail slipped over the side of the bed and dangled toward the floor.

THE FORTUNE

Billy assumed that Elinor had had a long talk with his wife, for after this brief illness when she was confined for two days to her bed and he was wholly excluded from the room and her presence, Frances was suddenly better – and much more like the Frances he married. She evidently was making an effort to pay more attention to him and Lilah. Her manner was no longer distracted. Her old shy smile returned sometimes. Billy returned to his wife's bed.

Her daily swims in the Perdido continued, but they only lasted about an hour. And she – and Elinor and Zaddie – no longer made a secret of them. One day Oscar said to Billy, 'When Elinor and I were first married, Elinor swam in the Perdido every day. Mama didn't take to that. In fact, no one in town took to that. But Elinor went ahead and did it, and I didn't say a word except, "Elinor, did you have a good swim today?" And Billy, maybe that's what you should say to Frances. 'Cause whether you like it or not, that's what Frances is gone do.'

Billy did not oppose the daily swims. It gradually became known in the town that Frances Bronze swam in that dangerous current just as her mother had many years before. People shook their heads and wondered at it, but the Caskeys were rich. They could do whatever they wanted.

Billy told himself that he should be satisfied now; every couple goes through a period of adjustment in marriage. His and Frances's adjustment hadn't been as wracking or as protracted as some he knew of. Yet Billy was pricked with the uneasy feeling that this Frances Caskey now sharing his bed wasn't the Frances Caskey he had married. It seemed to him that she was *acting* the part of a wife and mother. Her care of Lilah appeared to come only with conscious thought, as if she were consulting a spiral notebook with lists of things to be done in the proper raising of a child. Her timidly amorous advances to him in bed at night might have been approved by a printed calendar distributed by pharmacists. It was as if her very conversation and moods were calculated to provide the verisimilitude of normality.

There were times that Billy felt he *did* see the true Frances. Once when he returned home in the middle of the day to get some papers from Elinor he met his wife in the lower hallway. The day was chilly, but she was barefooted, bareheaded, and naked beneath her loosely gathered robe, having just come in from her swim. When he first saw her, she was smiling and radiant. But the smile faded the moment she glimpsed him in the dimness of the corridor.

On some evenings, when Billy and Oscar and other members of the family sat talking on the upstairs screened-in porch, he'd look through the window of his and Frances's room and see Frances seated before the vanity with Elinor behind her, softly brushing and arranging her daughter's hair. Their voices were low and musical, but Billy never learned of their conversations.

Billy became so accustomed to the new Frances that he began to forget the old one. Though he was working constantly with Miriam, they never said anything further about their conversation in Houston during which Miriam had told Billy she would marry him if Frances divorced him. Billy seemed to have two wives, the two Caskey sisters: Frances, who remained at home, raised his child, and saw to his clothes and lay in bed beside him at night, and Miriam, who talked to him on the telephone half a dozen times a day and made business trips with him, shared his work, and his financial interests. Neither woman was jealous of the prerogatives of the other. Billy wondered if this didn't represent perfection in a man's life, and concluded, as the months passed, that it did.

*

Late in October 1948, oil rig machinery was brought from Texas to Pensacola by boat, and taken by barge up the Perdido River. South of Gavin Pond Farm, as Elinor had showed Miriam more than a year ago, the swampland owned by the Caskeys was separated from the river by only a thin line of marsh grass and cypress. During times of heavy rainfall, these hammocks were overwhelmed and the swamp poured its excess water directly into the river. With great difficulty and the assistance of more than a hundred cursing, mosquito-bitten roustabouts imported from Louisiana, the machinery was taken into the interior of the swamp to an island that Miriam guaranteed – with Elinor's assurance – was never inundated. Drilling on the first well was begun in January 1949. Oil was struck within the week.

A second well, sunk a quarter of a mile away and nearer to Gavin Pond Farm, struck oil on the third day.

The oil industry was astonished. Miriam was not a geologist. Miriam was not even experienced in the business. But her drilling maps were uncannily accurate. When questioned, Miriam only smiled and said, 'I *always* know what I'm doing.' She never told that *her* directions came from Elinor.

Grace and Lucille were proud of the flares of burning gas that illuminated their nighttime sky to the south, visible out their bedroom window and from their bed. Not mincing words, Grace said, 'You know what that means, Lucille? That means money, money, money, money, money.'

A channel was cleared through the swamp to allow access for small barges that collected the oil that was pumped out. This was easier, it was thought, than building a causeway through the swamp and taking the oil out by truck. A third and then a fourth well were drilled from platforms built in the middle of the swamp. There was now no doubt in anyone's mind that these would strike oil as well.

Perdido watched all these events with astonishment. Oil lay under Texas and Oklahoma and Louisiana. It did not lie under Alabama or Florida. It was one thing for Grace and Lucille to set up a windmill on Gavin Pond Farm, but another thing altogether for them to sink an oil well on their property.

When the machinery-laden barges, the roustabouts, the engineers and foremen, the dredgers, the mechanics, the cooks, and all the other assorted hangers-on began to arrive in Escambia County, Florida, it was big news throughout the Alabama and Florida panhandles. Oil had been discovered here. And oil, everyone knew, was more valuable than cattle, pecans, and long-leaf yellow pine. Oil could make a man rich, if he happened to own land on which it was found. One didn't have to wait thirty years for a pecan tree to grow to maturity. One didn't have to buy feed for cattle. One didn't have to plant seedlings in careful rows and worry about insects and forest fires. One simply signed a piece of paper, and then deposited checks drawn on Texas banks. Oil was the preferred wealth of the lazy man. A man with oil money was respected by his neighbors in a way that a man with hard-earned and hard-kept money was not.

In two weeks, the small amount of available property along either side of the Perdido River from the town of Perdido itself all the way south to the Gulf of Mexico quintupled in price. The federal government owned much of the land on the eastern bank of the river. The western bank was forest land, and over half was owned by the Caskeys. Some farmers fortunate enough to own little homesteads of fifty or sixty acres sold them for forty or fifty thousand dollars, and immediately moved into Bay Minette or Foley and basked in their liberation from the obstinate Baldwin County soil. Other farmers decided to hold on to their farms. If the price of land had quintupled in two weeks, what might it not do in six weeks or a year?

Miriam was well regarded by her family. What pleased the Caskeys was not that she had persuaded Texas National Oil to bring their men and their machinery to that godforsaken swamp twenty miles from nowhere and to give the Caskeys money for what would have been no good to anybody anyhow, but rather that she had taken care – before any of this other came about – to make sure that the proceeds would be evenly distributed among the members of the family. The swampland was held in common by the Caskeys: that was why so many signatures were required and why so many power-of-attorney cards were on file with the bank and lawyers. When the oil started flowing, Billy distributed checks. Everyone in the family – Billy and Miriam included – was astonished by the size of those drafts. By the autumn of 1949, when the wells had been pumped only nine months, the Caskeys' income was greater from leasing royalties than it was from the entire profit of the mills.

'I don't know why we're working at all,' Oscar said, staring at an enormous check. 'We could close down the mill and sit back and relax.'

'And put six hundred people out of work,' Miriam pointed out. 'And make us all lazy and fat.'

'I'm lazy and fat already,' her father argued.

Miriam made no reply.

After receiving the checks from Billy, the Caskeys always just endorsed them and handed them back. 'What are we supposed to *do* with money like that?' Queenie demanded. 'I couldn't spend all that money if I was to work seven days a week at it. Billy, you go on and invest it somewhere.'

Billy laughed. 'Queenie, if I invest it, you're just going to make more.'

'All right,' said Queenie, 'so don't tell me about it. Just go ahead and do it.'

As the oil wells in the swamp continued to pump, and as other wells were sunk, the Caskeys grew accustomed to the new wealth, though they never quite grasped the meaning of such overweening prosperity. Queenie, for instance, judged all sums as fractions or multiples of twenty-nine dollars, which had been the cost, in 1943, of a new dress. A check for one hundred sixteen thousand dollars would purchase four thousand new dresses, and Queenie couldn't even begin to imagine closets to hold such a wardrobe as that. The limit of her imagination was a new car every year; anything beyond that exhausted her mind.

Miriam continued to run the mill, and Miriam and Billy together guided the Caskeys through the machinations of the oil companies and the exploitation of the swamp. There were trips now not only to Houston, but to New Orleans, Atlanta, and New York as well – sometimes by airplane. The Caskeys were rich, and their investments became more complicated. In whatever city Miriam visited, she always picked up some bijou made of diamonds, pearls, or colored gems to put in one of her safety-deposit boxes – she now had seven altogether. But even when she and Billy went out to a nightclub together on one of their trips, she never wore any jewels except the diamond bobs that had belonged to Mary-Love.

In the first years of this new financial grandeur, the Caskeys did not change the way Perdido thought they might. The greatest difference was in Oscar Caskey, who gave up his work at the mill. He ceased to take any interest whatsoever in the business except for the maintenance of the forests themselves. He still loved the smell of growing pine, he said. When Lake Pinchona opened a nine-hole golf course, Oscar took up the game, and played eighteen, twenty-seven, or even thirty-six holes every afternoon. He soon lost the fat he had gained in the past few years. He slept later in the mornings, and after his shave in the barbershop, he sometimes lingered around the back room of the establishment in hope of getting up a domino game. Miriam did not even pretend that he was needed at the mill. When she wanted his advice or opinion, she asked for it, but said otherwise, 'Go on Oscar, do what you like, we'll get along here just fine.'

Oscar heard of a fine golf course over near Tallahassee and had Bray drive him over early one morning. He made up a foursome in the clubhouse, and played all afternoon. The following week he returned and stayed for three days, playing morning and afternoon, this time taking Malcolm along for company. In time Oscar heard of other courses, some even farther away than Tallahassee, but he visited them anyway. Bray always drove him, and always in the back seat was the folded-up feather mattress he had so much missed the night he had been forced to spend out at Gavin Pond Farm. Oscar was rich and set in his ways. He loved to travel; he never went without his bed.

Elinor refused to go with him. She didn't like to be away from Perdido, she said. She couldn't bear leaving Frances and Lilah alone. Elinor and Frances were always in each other's company – except during Frances's daily swim in the Perdido.

Increased wealth did nothing to improve Sister's temper. She still kept to her bed. While originally the bed had been an excuse to get away from Early, Early had now become an excuse to remain in the bed. It no longer mattered that at first her contention that she could not walk had been a mere falsehood to keep her safe from Early Haskew; Sister's legs had withered. Now she most definitely could *not* walk, and she smugly considered her husband's loneliness in his house in Mobile with all the day lilies in the back yard.

Also, at the same time, for lack of anything better to occupy herself with, Sister picked a fight with Ivey Sapp. She accused Ivey of crippling her with the contents of the blue bottle she had swallowed on the night that Early Haskew had come to take her away. Ivey said in reply, 'You know what was in that bottle, Sister. You know it made you blind – that's all. You couldn't see and you fell down the stairs. And next morning you could see fine again. Don't try and tell me I had anything to do with your legs!' But Sister maintained her stance, and Ivey no more went upstairs. Queenie was needed all the more then.

Queenie was sixty, but lively and proud of her family. She rather wondered at her good fortune. There had been a time not so long ago when it had seemed that she had lost all three of her children to distance, disaster, or disappointment. Danjo was firmly entrenched in his castle in Germany now, that was true. But she had Malcolm to take up his place at the table. And here was she, possessing more money than she had ever dreamed it possible for any one human being to be possessed of, able to give Malcolm and Lucille cars and new clothes and little trips and big trips – anything in the world, in fact, that they wanted or would make them happy. Was there ever an aging woman who was happier than Queenie Strickland?

Malcolm was the Caskeys' workhorse, commanded to do many tasks, which he performed with ever-increasing facility. And it was apparent to everyone that Malcolm was in love with Miriam. Once, in her office at the mill, Malcolm looked up from some figures he was totaling for her, and said, 'Miriam, you want to get married?'

'To who?' Miriam asked, *not* looking up.

'To me,' said Malcolm.

'Why you want to get married to me?'

'I don't know. Just 'cause, I guess.'

'No,' said Miriam. 'If we got married, where would we live? We couldn't live with Queenie. She grates on my nerves, always has. And you couldn't live with me, 'cause you grate on Sister's nerves. Sister wouldn't even let me bring you in the house. That's why we cain't get married.'

This odd refusal of marriage made sense to Malcolm, and he never raised the subject again. He'd wait for Queenie – or for Sister – to die.

Roxie, who had remained with Queenie after James's death, died. Her fifty-year-old daughter, Reta, who remembered helping Miss Elinor scrub James's floor after the flood of 1919, came to Queenie's assistance. At Gavin Pond Farm, Sammy Sapp had a little brother and a little sister who could pick up pecans and put them in a sack before they could properly walk. Ivey and Zaddie had a fight in 1950 – about what, no one knew – and by 1954, though they continued to work in Elinor's kitchen together every day of the year, they still did not speak to each other. Bray's eyes failed, and his job as chauffeur was handed over to a younger man, the husband of yet another of the Sapp daughters.

At Gavin Pond Farm, Grace and Lucille got along as well as they ever had, and Tommy Lee was growing up in the constant company of Sammy Sapp, Luvadia's boy. Grace put Tommy Lee on the tractor for the first time when he was four, and showed him how to steer. Because his feet wouldn't reach the pedals, she placed a large rock on the accelerator and allowed him to till a recently cleared field. With the money coming in from the oil, Grace bought two of the best bulls in the country and opened a stud service. She built two barns, a stable, and a silo. And she doubled the size of the house with the addition of a living room, three bedrooms, two baths, and a playroom for Tommy Lee. She bought horses for herself and Lucille and a pony for Tommy Lee. She had a catfish pond scooped out of the earth and graveled the road from the Babylon highway. They began to entertain, and Thanksgiving for the Caskeys was held out at the farm instead of at Elinor's. Grace and Lucille were hosts of a vast New Year's Eve party. They invited everybody they knew from Perdido, Babylon, and Pensacola. Grace had a houseboat specially constructed for her in Pensacola which she moored on the bank of the Perdido and where she and Lucille went when they wanted to be alone. Grace's great itch remained the acquisition of land, and she unmercifully badgered owners of property next to the farm. With the backup of ever-increasing oil revenues, her offers increased steadily until they were irresistible, and every year Gavin Pond Farm's fences lengthened. By 1955 it was the largest private landholding in the Florida panhandle.

*

What was good for the Caskeys was good for the entire area. Now oil companies began to look at the area on both banks of the Perdido. Other wells were drilled, some on Caskey property. More than half struck oil; *more* money poured into the region.

With the prosperity of the Caskey mills and oil enterprises the population of Perdido doubled to more than five thousand. The Caskeys bought the pecan orchard and cattle pasture across the road from their houses so that it could not be built upon. The town expanded south along both banks of the Perdido and west into the pine forest. The Caskeys relinquished some of their land near the town for building. More shops opened downtown, and their quality rivaled those in Pensacola and Mobile. Perdido society, with more money in its pocket, began to dress up. Little parties were arranged to go to Mobile for the evening. Rented railroad cars transported carousers to the Auburn–Alabama game in the fall. Beach houses were erected at Destin or Gulf Shores. Lake Pinchona became the Perdido Country Club. With money lent at low interest by Oscar, the country club added another nine holes to its golf course.

The town seemed overrun with children. The grammar school expanded with funds donated by the Caskeys. A municipal swimming pool was installed next to the high school, and now no one in Perdido need be tempted to swim in the Perdido or the Blackwater. There was even talk of repairing the levee, which had developed visible cracks and had eroded away in a few places, although no one remembered the last time the water had been high enough to threaten the town. In recent years the rivers behind their walls of clay had been placid, and it seemed a waste of money to recondition the levees when two faces of the town hall clock didn't keep correct time and so many streets in Baptist Bottom were not paved.

Miriam was revered in Perdido for having brought prosperity to the area. In Babylon and other towns of Escambia County, Florida, Grace was given the credit. Whenever she went to the seed and feed store in Babylon she was besieged. Men thanked her for what she had done; men asked for the names of the top people at Texas National Oil; men offered to sell her their land for sums that staggered her. She liked these men and wished them success; her great fortune made her want the same for others.

One day in the store Grace ran into a farmer she had known for several years. He was a hard-working churchgoer. His wife had died of pneumonia two years back and he had always known bad luck. He said to her, 'Well, Miz Caskey, you know where my place is, my boy and I have about two hundred acres right down there between Cantonement and Muscogee. We raise a little soybean, raise a little corn. Make a little money when there's rain, lose a little money when there's not. Well, my boy and me was standing out in the field one day, saw this machinery on the other side of the fence – not our property – talked to the men there, found out they was looking for oil. And they was finding it! So we just took down our fence there, and we said: "Y'all come on through!" And they did, and they found oil. I wasn't surprised. Somebody come up to my boy yesterday and says, "What's the soybean crop gone be like this year?" And my boy says, "Hell, I don't know why you're asking me – we don't raise soybean no more. We got machinery on our land, and we don't plant soybean, 'cause the roots might go down and disturb the machinery." You don't hardly make money on soybean anyway. We raise oil now. Not hardly no comparison between the two, so far as money goes. We don't even have to run that machinery. All we have to do is slit open them checks every month. We have bought us two pick-'em-up trucks. Drove up to Atmore to get 'em, and we had our choice so we bought two of 'em that look just alike. That damn oil is flowing like a artesian well . . .'

The Caskeys owned one thousand times this farmer's two hundred acres of oil-rich land.

LEGACIES

Everyone in the town knew that a strangeness had grown between Frances Bronze and her husband Billy. Some said Billy was having an affair with his sister-in-law Miriam. Those who knew the Caskeys better discounted this information on three counts. First of all: 'Billy wouldn't do it.' He was upright, God-fearing, and wholly devoted to the Caskey family; he would never create a situation so destructive to family interests. The second argument was: 'Miriam wouldn't do it.' No one had ever known Miriam to be interested in anything but making money, buying jewelry, and speaking her mind without a moment's thought about consequence. So far as anyone had ever seen, Miriam had no interest in men. Those trips to Texas were strictly business, and besides, didn't Malcolm Strickland always go along? The third argument went: 'Elinor wouldn't have allowed it.' Everyone knew how deeply Elinor loved her daughter, knew how faithfully she had nursed Frances through her dreadful childhood illnesses, and knew that Elinor was fiercely protective of Frances. If Elinor had thought there was anything between Billy and Miriam she would have put a stop to it instantly.

Frances no longer denied the feelings that had taken root in her. She was devoted to 'her other daughter,' Nerita. She lived for those hours spent in the water. Recognition only increased these feelings. Oscar, though distracted with thoughts of golf and travel, noticed his daughter's remoteness. Frances had withdrawn, not only from Billy, but from them all. 'Talk to her, Elinor,' Oscar said. 'Talk to her sometime when I'm not here.'

Oscar was gone somewhere every week it seemed, at one golf course or another; and he preferred those far away, in landscapes different from those of the Alabama panhandle. Billy was absent often, too, on business. When the women were left alone, their lives were quiet and circumscribed and formal. Elinor now insisted that the family dress for dinner at her home. Their enlarged fortune and expanding importance in the region required it, she said. Even Oscar, though it chafed, put on a coat and tie before he sat down at the table. Elinor invariably wore the black pearls.

Late in May 1956, Oscar was in Raleigh, North Carolina, visiting friends and the three excellent courses in the area. Miriam and Billy and Malcolm were in New Orleans. Queenie had accompanied Grace and Lucille to a cattle auction in Georgia. Sister took her meals alone. Elinor, Frances, and Lilah ate dinner in splendor in the dining room, waited on by Zaddie in a starched black uniform.

Nine-year-old Lilah chatted with her grandmother, telling her about the end of the school year and the party that was planned for the country club and what she wanted to do during the summer. Frances sat by, quietly eating, not exactly ignoring her daughter, but apparently oblivious to her. After dessert, Elinor said to Lilah, 'Darling, why don't you go upstairs for a little while? Your mama and I need to do a little talking.'

Lilah, on the condition that Elinor allow her to sit at her vanity and try on her jewelry, assented.

'Mama?' the child asked, turning to Frances.

Frances looked up suddenly. 'What, dear?'

'Mama,' said Lilah slowly, with the air of imparting a lesson to a backward child, 'may I be excused?'

'Yes, of course,' said Frances absently.

After Lilah had left the room, Elinor called in Zaddie. 'Bring us some more coffee, Zaddie, and then close the doors, please.' Zaddie did so.

Elinor sat silent and erect at the head of the table, fingering the black pearls gleaming dimly in the candlelight. Frances also sat quietly, her head slightly averted, gazing through the gauze curtains at the deep blackness of the pine forest beyond the edge of the property. A wind had sprung up in the last hour, and it was laden with moisture, portending heavy rain. The curtains blew about and the candles guttered.

'Mama?' said Frances, without concern. 'What did you want to talk about?'

'You're unhappy,' said Elinor simply. 'It hurts me to see you unhappy. It hurts me very much.'

Frances toyed with her coffee spoon, moving it slowly around the rim of her cup with its cooling, untasted coffee. 'Yes,' said Frances at last, 'I am unhappy, I guess.'

'Why?'

'Because I don't know who I am,' said Frances quickly, and then glanced at her mother with surprise.

'What do you mean – *who you are*?'

'I feel like I'm losing touch,' said Frances.

'With Billy?'

'With everything,' returned Frances solemnly. 'With Billy, with Lilah, with Daddy – with this house, with Perdido and money and clothes. With just about everything.'

'With me?' asked Elinor.

Frances smiled, reached out and squeezed her mother's hand on the cut-work linen tablecloth.

'No,' whispered Frances, 'not with you. Everything is – I don't know how to put this, Mama – *vague*, like I'm going blind or something. Fuzzy. Pale. And I hear the same way, too – fuzzy. That's why everything has to be said to me twice before I say anything back. At first I thought maybe I should go see the doctor . . .'

Elinor waved this away.

'I know,' said Frances. 'Besides, it's not *everything* that's so vague to me. See, *you're* not. I see you, and I hear you talk – except when you're talking to Billy or Daddy or Lilah or somebody – and you're just the way you always were.'

'What do you think it is?' asked Elinor.

'I know what it is,' returned Frances. 'And you do, too.'

Elinor nodded.

'You didn't tell me about this part,' said Frances.

'I didn't know about it,' said Elinor. 'I didn't know it would happen.'

Frances smiled wanly. 'But it has. All this' – she waved her hand about the dining room, as if she meant it to encompass all of her life – 'is fading, Mama. And you know what's become real?'

'Nerita?'

Frances nodded. 'That's my real life, the time I spend with her.' Frances looked up at the ceiling. 'Lilah – she's not my little girl. She belongs to you much more than she does to me. Poor thing, I feel so sorry for her, because her real mama doesn't love her the way she should. Lilah's not my real little girl. My real little girl is out there in the Perdido. I worry about *her*. I think about *her*. You know why I never go off with Billy? You know why I never go off with Daddy? Because I couldn't stand to be away from my little girl for a single day. Mama, I live for that hour in the water every afternoon.'

'I know you do.'

'And you know what I've found out?'

'What?' asked Elinor apprehensively.

'That even that one hour a day is too much. It's harder and harder for me to change back. Sometimes I have to sit out on the edge of the river covering myself up with a blanket. One time Zaddie came out there looking for me, but I couldn't stand up because she would have seen. And soon, Mama, what's gone happen is that I won't be able to go out in the water for even five minutes without that change keeping on for longer and longer.'

'And that's why you're unhappy.'

Frances nodded. 'What if I had to stop seeing Nerita? It would kill me. Oh, Mama, do you *know* how happy we are down there?'

Elinor nodded with a smile, and pushed away her coffee cup. 'I've seen you. You are as happy with Nerita as I was with you. Darling, I love you! I love you so much! It *kills* me to see you like this.'

'Then tell me what to do, Mama.'

'I don't know what you can do.'

'Then just tell me what's going to happen.'

There was a sudden clap of thunder. A moment later, rain began to fall. Its scent invaded the room and the candles cowered beneath the dampness.

The rain fell so hard that Elinor had to raise her voice to be heard over it. 'I don't know what's going to happen.'

The rain continued throughout that evening. Frances and Elinor eventually went upstairs. They looked in on Lilah, who sat contented at the vanity, clipping diamond earrings to her ears.

'You should have been Miriam's little girl,' laughed Frances, 'not mine. Someday you should get Miriam to open one of her safety-deposit boxes for you.'

'I've already asked her,' said Lilah, expertly clasping a gold necklace at the back of her neck. 'Are y'all still talking?'

'Yes, ma'am,' said Elinor. 'Do you mind?'

'Do I have to get out?'

'No,' said Elinor. 'We'll go across the hall.' Frances sat at *her* vanity, and Elinor took down her daughter's hair and began to brush it. The rain blew through the open window, soaking the curtains and dripping onto the carpet.

'Do you want me to close that?' Elinor asked.

Frances shrugged and was silent. She seemed lost in her own thoughts as her head was tugged this way and that by Elinor's stern movements with the brush.

At last, Frances looked up at her mother's reflection in the mirror. 'Mama,' said Frances softly, 'what if I went back?'

'Back?' Elinor echoed. The arm holding the brush trembled and dropped to her side.

'Went back forever,' Frances went on.

'It wouldn't be *going back*, exactly,' said Elinor cautiously. 'Because you never really lived there.'

'Yes, but I could live there, couldn't I?'

Elinor didn't answer this directly. 'What about Billy?'

Frances smiled. 'Would you throw him out?'

'Of course not. We all love Billy.'

'Then Billy will be fine. Billy didn't want to marry *me*, he just wanted to marry this family. If you let him stay on, he'd be happy. Maybe Miriam would marry him,' Frances mused.

'What about Oscar? What about Lilah?' demanded Elinor, going to the window and slamming it down in its sash.

'Daddy will miss me,' Frances conceded. 'But Lilah won't. I'll leave her my jewels.' Frances flipped open the top of her jewelry case and plunged her fingers in. She withdrew her hand slowly. A bracelet and a single earring slipped to the carpet, but Frances apparently didn't notice.

'What about *me*?' Elinor asked at last.

'Mama,' laughed Frances, 'you can *visit*.'

Elinor looked around the room. 'Wouldn't you miss everybody? Wouldn't you miss everything you've always had? What if you got down there and didn't like it, didn't like the Perdido for twenty-four hours a day, seven days a week?'

'Mama,' said Frances, following her mother's gaze about the room, 'this has been my room for thirty-five years, but it just doesn't feel like home. That river does.'

Elinor sat down on the edge of her daughter's bed. 'When would you go?' she asked.

Frances glanced out the window. Lightning struck nearby and illuminated the tops of the water oaks in the sandy yards.

'Tonight,' said Frances. 'Why not tonight?' She rose from the vanity. 'Unhook me, Mama,' she said, with obvious excitement. 'Help me undress.'

'You can't—'

'Tonight is perfect,' said Frances. 'I'll just wait till Lilah is in bed.'

'What will I tell Billy, what will—'

'Tell everybody I drowned.' Frances shrugged. 'Everybody in Perdido has been expecting it for years.' She walked to the window and raised it. She thrust her head out into the stormy night. Lightning exploded and thunder shook the house. Frances withdrew her head. Her hair was soaked, and rain streamed down her face.

'That hit the levee!' she laughed. 'I saw it strike!'

She pulled off her earrings and dropped them on the vanity.

'All this stuff goes to Lilah. She'll like it. I never did. Grace is about my size. Let her go through my closet. Everything else goes to the church in Baptist Bottom.'

Frances smiled as she said all this; her eyes sparkled.

Lilah pushed open the door of the room. 'It's really coming down,' she said. 'I closed all the windows up here.'

She glanced with disapproval at the open window and the puddle of water forming on the edge of the carpet.

'Mama,' she said reproachfully, 'didn't you even *notice*?'

Frances only laughed. She threw herself down on the bench before the vanity and called Lilah over to her. Lilah edged closer.

Frances reached out and grabbed Lilah. She hugged her and laughed.

'Mama!' protested the little girl, who had rarely been embraced by her mother.

Elinor sat glumly on the edge of the bed and stared at her daughter. Her glance was not lost on Lilah.

'Mama, are you all right?' the girl asked cautiously, drawing back from her mother.

Frances grinned, swept up the earrings she had taken off, and clipped them to Lilah's ears.

'Ouch!' cried Lilah.

'They're yours!'

Lilah drew in her breath sharply, and held it. Swiveling around, she looked at her grandmother with an expression that said, *Can I keep them?*

Elinor nodded yes.

Frances laughed again, picked up the entire jewelry box and thrust it into her daughter's hands.

'You want these, too?'

Lilah backed away.

Frances shrugged, laughed, and stood up. She waved her arms before her. 'Go to bed, go to bed! It's late!'

In mute wonder, with her hands over the emerald bobs on her ears, Lilah backed out of her mother's bedroom. She ran across the hall to her bedroom and slammed the door shut.

The storm abated for a bit, then returned with greater force. Perdido closed its windows, pulled its curtains drawn, and turned up the volume on its television sets. An oak sapling on the Baptist Bottom levee was struck with lightning and burst into flames, burning a few seconds before the torrential rain snuffed it out like an ignited match plunged into a cistern full of water.

At eleven o'clock, Perdido went to its windows, looked out, and wondered that the storm didn't stop.

Small trenches appeared in the earth around foundations, dug by the cascade of water falling from roofs. Gutters were overwhelmed. Perdido felt the first twinges of uneasiness over the fact that, in three decades, no municipal funds had been spent on the maintenance of the levees. The rivers would no doubt rise.

Children trembled in their beds, bracing for the next burst of thunder. With flashlights their parents searched out leaks, wearily placing buckets and pans beneath them.

Elinor's house was quiet. Lilah was asleep. Zaddie lay in bed reading old copies of *Coronet* and listening as the rain beat against the low sloping roof of the lattice.

At the very peak of the storm, with lightning crackling across the sky for long seconds, sharp blasts of thunder lasting for what seemed like minutes, and rain falling in heavy sheets, two figures appeared on the front porch of the Caskey mansion at the edge of the town. No one saw them.

Frances was clad in a loose dark robe. Her mother wore a long dark raincoat. Both women were barefoot.

Frances looked at her mother for a moment. Then she leaned forward and threw her arms about Elinor. She squeezed tightly and Elinor squeezed back.

Frances stepped through the veil of black water that poured thunderously from the roof of the house.

She paused at the foot of the steps and looked back up.

Elinor stepped boldly through the curtain of water, descended the steps, and grasped her daughter's hand.

Together, they made their way around the house and into the shadow and protection of the water oaks. Neither glanced at the lighted window of Sister's room next door, as they walked slowly toward the levee. In such darkness and heavy rain as this, they were confident they'd never be seen. They mounted the steps behind Queenie's house, stood for a few moments on the top of the clay embankment, and gazed down into the swiftly flowing black waters of the Perdido, its surface a wide dark ribbon of turbulence.

Frances again embraced her mother. When she drew away, Elinor plucked the robe from her daughter's shoulders and allowed it to fall in the red mud atop the levee. Frances stood naked.

Frances glanced once more at her mother, saying nothing. She did not touch her, but stepped to the side of the levee that sloped down to the river, then went sliding down past blackberry brambles, past saplings, past broken bottles and clumps of kudzu roots till she reached the bottom.

Elinor peered down. An enormous bolt of lightning illuminated the entire sky, and Elinor saw her daughter descend into the water. Before she went completely under, Frances raised one hand in brief farewell.

Elinor remained at the top of the levee for half an hour. The lightning and thunder had moved northward, but the rain was still heavy. The night was darker. Finally she walked slowly down the concrete steps and across the yard. After bathing each foot in the curtain of water falling from the roof of the house, she went inside and roused Zaddie to tell her of Frances's drowning in the night water of the Perdido.

Continue the story in

BLACKWATER VI
RAIN

ABOUT THE AUTHOR

Michael McDowell was born in 1950 in Enterprise, Alabama and attended public schools in southern Alabama until 1968. He graduated with a bachelor's degree and a master's degree in English from Harvard, and in 1978 he was awarded his Ph.D. in English and American Literature from Brandeis.

His seventh novel written and first to be sold, *The Amulet*, was published in 1979 and would be followed by over thirty additional volumes of fiction written under his own name or the pseudonyms Nathan Aldyne, Axel Young, Mike McCray, and Preston MacAdam. His notable works include the Southern Gothic horror novels *Cold Moon Over Babylon* (1980) and *The Elementals* (1981), the serial novel *Blackwater* (1983), which was first published in a series of six paperback volumes, and the trilogy of *Jack & Susan* books.

By 1985 McDowell was writing screenplays for television, including episodes for a number of anthology series such as *Tales from the Darkside*, *Tales from the Crypt*, and *Alfred Hitchcock Presents*. He went on to write the screenplays for Tim Burton's *Beetlejuice* (1988) and *The Nightmare Before Christmas* (1993), as well as the script for *Thinner* (1996). McDowell died in 1999 from AIDS-related illness. Tabitha King, wife of author Stephen King, completed an unfinished McDowell novel, *Candles Burning*, which was published in 2006.

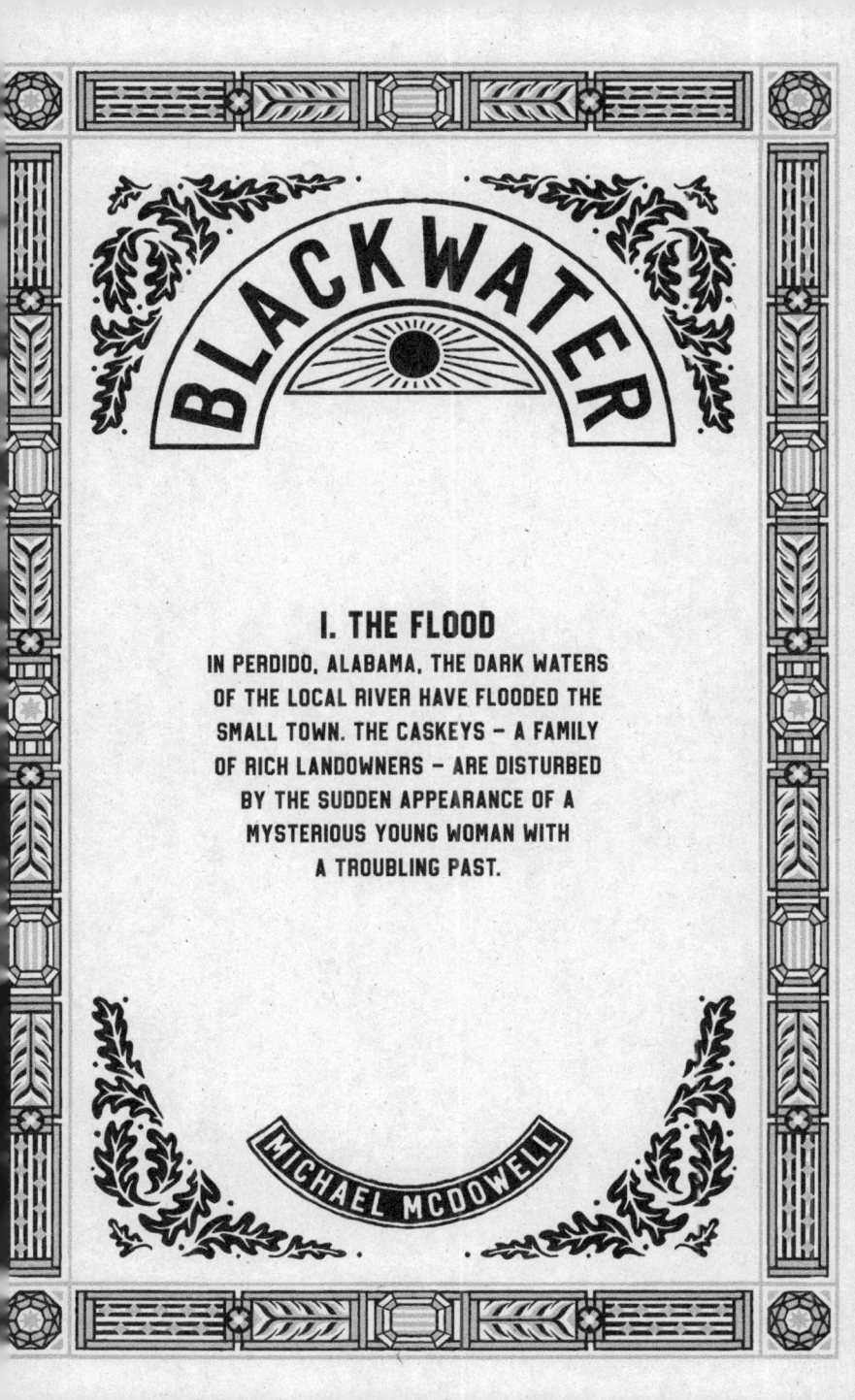

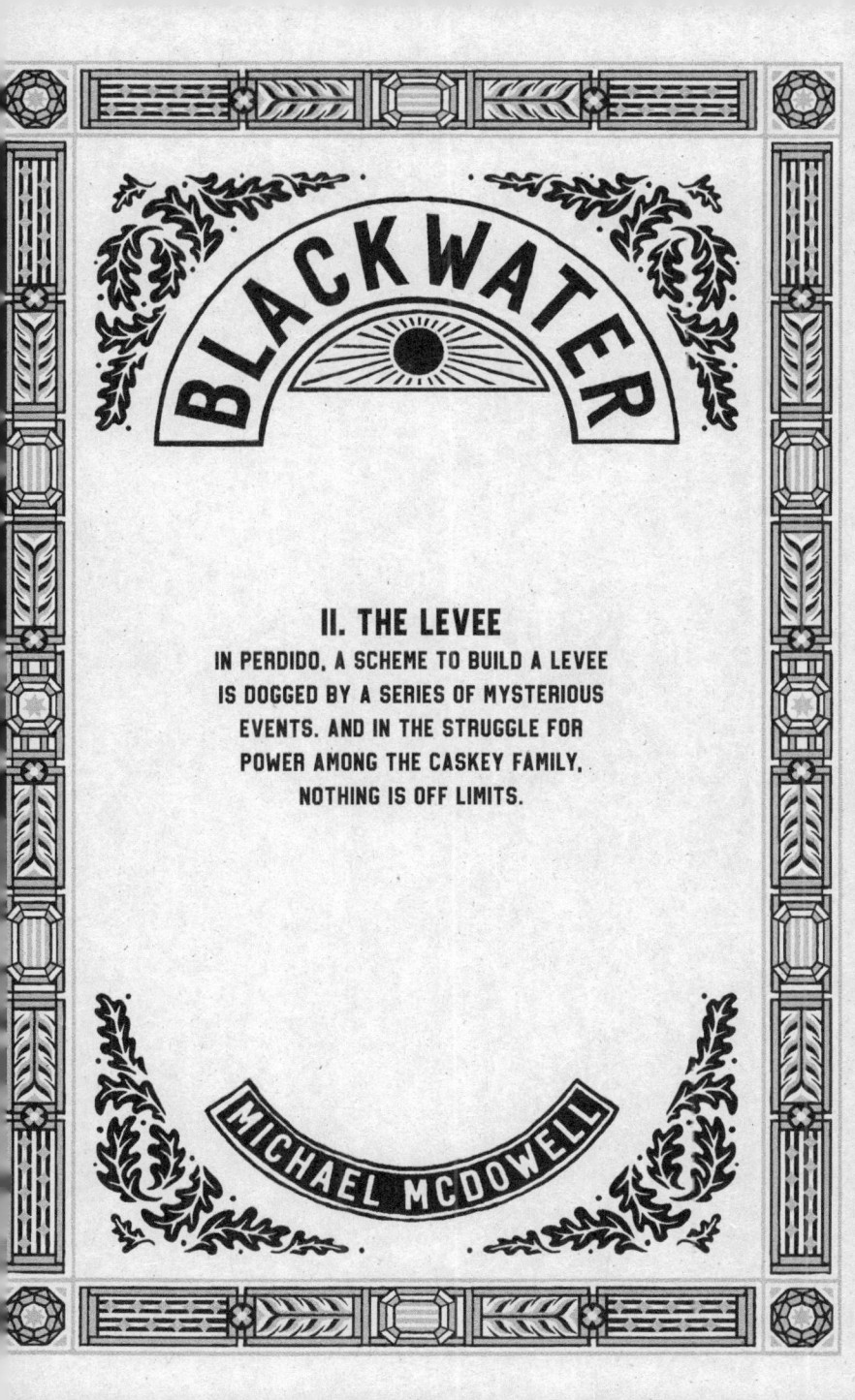